DISCOVERY

Suddenly the lights went out plunging the windowless hall into darkness. There was a woman's high-pitched squeal, followed by other voices.

"What's going on? Somebody turn on the lights!"

Tess found a counter and ran her hand along it until she felt the metal cash box. At least she knew where she was now. She'd found the Drunkard's Path booth. As she took a few more cautious steps into the booth her shin hit something solid. One of the partitions had fallen. She felt suddenly cold. It couldn't have fallen by itself.

Abruptly, light flooded the hall and there was a communal sigh of relief. Tess saw that the far side of the partition rested on the floor, but the part she had bumped into was a good two feet off the ground. A hunter green corner of the Drunkard's Path quilt stuck out from one corner. Luke stepped forward and righted the partition and then looked down and halted, frozen to the spot by what he saw.

"Good God," he said.

DEATH
ON THE
DRUNKARD'S
PATH

An Iris House Mystery

JEAN HAGER

AVON BOOKS ◆ NEW YORK

AVON BOOKS
A division of
The Hearst Corporation
1350 Avenue of the Americas
New York, New York 10019

Copyright © 1996 by Jean Hager
Inside cover author photo by *Rocky Mountain News*/Steve Groer
Published by arrangement with the author
Library of Congress Catalog Card Number: 95-94912
ISBN: 0-380-77211-6

First Avon Books Printing: April 1996

AVON TRADEMARK REG. U.S. PAT. OFF. AND IN OTHER COUNTRIES, MARCA REGISTRADA, HECHO EN U.S.A.

Printed in the U.S.A.

RA 10 9 8 7 6 5 4 3 2 1

Chapter 1

Rex Brindle draped the last of his one-of-a-kind contemporary quilts over a black and silver folding screen, artfully arranging it to display the intricate pieced work. Celestial Bodies was one of his finest creations. It contained shades of blue, from ice-blue to navy so deep it looked black, with yellows, from the palest cream to deep gold; and its tiny hand stitches were sewn with metallic gold thread.

In Rex's unhumble opinion, Celestial Bodies was a masterpiece, an absolutely inspired work of art.

He stepped back several feet to admire his booth, which was filled with the most unusual and expensive pieces of quilt art to be found anywhere. Rex's quilts were in great demand and all sold for four figures. Even the wall hangings, which were about half the size of bed quilts, commanded a thousand dollars. And he already had a buyer for Celestial Bodies, a folk art museum willing to pay ten thousand dollars.

Rex rubbed his palms together in irrepressible glee. The sale to the museum would be his first five-figure sale, the first of many, he fervently hoped.

Glancing to his right, he caught sight of his reflection in a mirror attached to the next booth, which offered for sale quilted collars, vests, and jackets. His

1

lean face with pointed chin and black hair parted in the middle and swept back in crow's wings contributed to a devilish appearance.

Grinning, he gave himself a congratulatory thumbs up sign. Rex did not suffer from an inferiority complex. Frankly, he considered himself an artistic genius, and eventually he felt sure the entire art world would recognize it, too. None of those three-hundred-dollar Irish Chains or Grandmother's Flower Gardens for Rex Brindle! As for allowing a sewing machine to touch a quilt, that was heresy! Every stitch in a Rex Brindle quilt was put in by his own clever, callused fingers.

Trained as an artist, he'd spent five years painting oil portraits and watercolor landscapes, while barely managing to keep body and soul together. In desperation, he'd turned to quilting, where men were still very much in the minority. It was the smartest decision he'd ever made. Now he earned a comfortable living selling his quilts and taking commissions at four quilt shows a year.

In addition, he received more invitations for workshops and demonstrations than he could possibly accept. It was an abundance of riches, and it saddened him that he couldn't grab it all like a greedy child, but he had to leave time for his work. Fortunately, he only required five hours of sleep a night.

He'd spent most of the day setting up his booth for tomorrow's opening, and his stomach was complaining that it had missed lunch and wanted dinner post haste. He'd try that steak house he'd noticed as he drove around town last evening, searching for Iris House Bed and Breakfast, where he was staying while in Victoria Springs.

But first, a quick run-through of the hall to check out the competition. There was plenty of it. Close to a hundred booth spaces had been rented, at least half of them offering quilts for sale. The annual Victoria Springs Quilt Show and

Sale was one of the largest in the region, attended by quilters and quilt lovers from a dozen states. There was even an interior decorator staying at Iris House, who'd come to shop for her clients. The little upstart had hinted that she'd like to buy one of Rex's creations, provided he would give her a twenty-five percent discount. He'd told her stiffly that he didn't have to discount his quilts.

To be sure he had the times fixed in his mind, Rex picked up one of the red flyers that were lying around the Civic Center Exhibition Hall and scanned it quickly.

Quilt Show and Sale
Victoria Springs, Missouri
Civic Center Exhibition Hall
Wednesday, Oct. 15–Sunday, Oct. 19
9 A.M.–6 P.M.
Workshops!
Demonstrations!
Raffles!
Sales Booths!
Ribbon Awards!
Drawings for Gift Certificates!
Among the country's best quilters and quilting teachers
who will share their expertise are: Rex Brindle,
Letitia Lattimore, Marlene Oxley, and Cassie Terhune

Since the four stars of the quilting world were listed alphabetically, Rex's name appeared first. He considered the order symbolic, for he had no doubt that he was also number one in ability, an artist first, a quilter second.

Sixtyish Letitia Lattimore was among the best of the older generation of traditional quilters. She even looked the part, like everybody's grandmother, who was probably baking cookies when she wasn't quilting. But Rex believed that traditional quilting stifled the imagination. The number of different pattern and color combinations one could come up with was limited, which was why poor, old Letitia, fine craftswoman though she was, would never be a great quilt artist. He had to admit that didn't seem to bother Letitia one whit. She didn't aspire to be more than she was.

Marlene Oxley, who would judge the work of local quilters entered in the competition and award ribbons to the winners, had gamely tried to break out of traditional quilting and create her own designs, most of which had been on a level with kindergarten fingerpainting, an outcome Rex could have predicted had anyone asked his opinion. Marlene was too repressed to give her imagination free rein. Wisely, she had returned to the old traditional patterns, specializing in applique work. Because of her meticulous needlework, Marlene's quilts sold well in the five- to six-hundred dollar range.

Sad to say, some people simply had to be content with mediocrity.

Cassie Terhune was another matter, Rex mused as he approached her booth. Rex would love to know what her annual income was. He feared it equaled or, heaven forbid, surpassed his own. Cassie had a weekly television quilting show and produced her own videos and books. She was virtually a one-woman factory. She'd left the high-powered world of corporate law to be a quilter, a fact few people were aware of. When Rex learned of Cassie's former occupation, he hadn't been at all surprised, for he had reason to know that the gracious manner and sweet smile Cassie affected for her students and clients hid a hardheaded business woman. He chuckled to himself. Cassie would turn pea-green when she heard what Rex's Celestial Bodies had sold for.

Since Cassie wasn't around, Rex took time to examine her booth with a critical eye. Some of the quilts were of Cassie's own design, quite ordinary, really, though she used color and varying sizes of blocks in the same quilt to make them appear more complex than they actually were. Clever, Rex admitted to himself, a ploy that worked for most people. But cleverness was not art, and Rex's artist's eye was not fooled.

Near the front of the booth, instructional quilting videos in bright-colored jackets were displayed on a table in a fan arrangement. Cassie Terhune smiled at him from every one of them, her mahogany-colored hair creating a halo around an oval face with gray eyes that crinkled at the corners. With back-lighting and special lens, the photographer had done wonders with that forty-seven-year-old face. Cassie didn't look a day over forty.

Cassie's quilting books were stacked by title on a second table. Rex counted four stacks and did a double-take. As far as he knew, Cassie had written only three books. He had all of them. He owned practically every quilting book published in the last five years. On the rare occasions when he feared his creative juices were drying up, all he had to do to assuage his doubt was page through a few of the books in his library. There wasn't a quilt in any of them that came up to his high standards. He always returned to his work, bolstered by the knowledge that Rex Brindle's quilts were in a class by themselves.

Upon closer scrutiny, he didn't recognize the cover on the book atop the stack nearest him. Clearly Cassie had a new volume fresh off the press, and that made four books in less than three years. How did she do it? Considering that she was involved in a TV show, teaching workshops, and a video and book production business, Rex was amazed that she had time for any actual quilting at all. But the quilts before his eyes seemed to be evidence that she did.

Of course, it hadn't taken a great burst of imagination to turn out any of them, Rex told himself with a curl of his upper lip. And if you looked closely you could see she'd used simple, quick-to-stitch designs for the actual quilting. She had probably gone from one to another without pause, while Rex sometimes spent weeks creating and refining various designs on his drawing board before finally deciding on a project. Even then, he often had to dye the fabrics himself to get exactly the right hues.

Nevertheless, time was finite—there were only so many days in a year. Frankly, Rex suspected Cassie had so many projects going that she must farm out the quilting itself to somebody else. Perhaps several somebodies, all of whom were undoubtedly sworn to secrecy. Cassie herself would never admit to such a subterfuge.

He imagined a poorly lighted sweatshop where women toiled long hours for a pittance, and chuckled to himself. Naw, it couldn't be that bad. But if he ever had proof that other people worked on quilts sold as Cassie Terhune's handiwork, he wouldn't hesitate to spread the word around. Selling others' work as your own was dishonest, like selling rip-off Rolex watches as the real thing.

He picked up one of the new books and thumbed through it. He was surprised, even a bit chagrined, to see that Cassie's designs were improving. Several of the quilts were actually quite attractive, even unique.

Whoa. What was this?

For a long moment, he stared at a beautiful full-page color photograph of Reflections of Sunlight, a quilt featuring a sunburst pattern, before his brain could register what his eyes were seeing.

Impossible!

His heart thudded. No, no, no. It couldn't be. Surely he was mistaken. He remained frozen to the spot until his breathing quieted. Then he turned to the back of the book where the pattern pages were located and found the pattern for Reflections of Sunlight.

As he stared at the pattern, he felt a hot rush of blood

to his face. A conundrum, to which he'd had no satisfactory explanation before now, was finally solved.

He had been puzzled by Cassie's visit to his Dallas studio with some of her students a year ago, and he'd left designs-in-progress scattered all over his desk and drawing board to show them around. After all, they'd traveled all the way from Kansas City, and he'd been secretly pleased at what he had taken as a compliment from a fellow quilter who had never been lavish with her praise for other people's work. Only afterward had it occurred to him to wonder what had motivated Cassie. The woman always had a hidden agenda.

Now the real reason for the visit lay before his eyes. And Cassie's lengthy disappearance from the tour group, because she was feeling ill, she'd said, was explained.

Rex turned from hot to cold with rage as he quickly glanced through the other patterns and recognized three more of them.

He couldn't believe it. The bitch had stolen his designs!

He slammed the book shut and threw it at the table, toppling the stack of offending volumes, several of which spilled on the floor. He could barely restrain himself from trampling them to smithereens beneath his feet. But prudence prevailed, and he left them, turned on his heel, and stormed across the exhibition hall.

The thief!

The two-faced, conniving sneak!

Cassie Terhune had played her dirty little game with the wrong person this time!

Nobody stole the product of Rex Brindle's colossal creative imagination and got away with it. This time she would pay the piper. At the moment, nothing Rex could think of seemed punishment severe enough. A ruined reputation. A lawsuit for actual and punitive damages. Boiling in oil.

Well, he would come up with something suitable. He would *destroy* her.

Chapter 2

Tess Darcy held up a Drunkard's Path quilt in hunter green and cream. Her auburn curls framed her oval face in tangled disarray and her tired brown eyes were scratchy from rubbing them with fingers contaminated by dye from the fabrics all around her.

Mary Franks backed off and studied the quilt Tess was holding, her chin in her hand, fingertips gently tapping her round cheek. The callused tips identified Mary as a serious quilter, all of whom, Tess had noticed, had calluses.

As president of Victoria Springs Quilters' Guild, Mary was in charge of the guild's demonstration booth. Each year, the guild exhibited quilts made by their members, using a single traditional quilt pattern in all its variations. This year, the pattern chosen by the guild was the Drunkard's Path and its variations, known as Falling Timbers, Fool's Puzzle, and Country Husband. The traditional Drunkard's Path block pattern was a simple one, consisting of only two pieces. One piece had a concave curved edge, the other a convex curved edge, which were joined to make a block. When the blocks were sewn together, they formed twisting paths that crossed each other in diagonal progress across the quilt.

Having always loved quilts, Tess had joined the guild when she took a Log Cabin quilt class at The Quilter's Nook, a local quilt shop. She'd finished the quilt top during the class. Using a quilter's rotary cutter to cut several strips of fabric at a time and a sewing machine to join them into blocks had made the work go quickly. She'd bought a lap-held hoop, quilting thread, and #8 needles, but had yet to find time to get started on the most time-consuming part, the hand quilting itself.

Sitting down to outline every strip in her queen-sized quilt with careful hand stitching was a daunting prospect, even if she had time to spare—which she rarely did. Running her Iris House Bed and Breakfast was a full-time job. On the infrequent occasions when she did find a spare hour or two, she seemed always to have something more pressing on hand—like doing her part for the guild. Feeling obligated to contribute her share, she had volunteered to help Mary prepare the booth for tomorrow's opening day of the quilt show.

"We want to make it stand out," Mary mused, still studying the quilt. A slightly plump, slow-speaking, middle-aged woman, Mary might appear lackadaisical, but she was hardworking and tended toward perfectionism. The quilt in question was a group project and would be raffled off during the show at a dollar a chance, the proceeds going to the guild's treasury. As Tess was holding the quilt with the back side to her, she had plenty of time to admire the ability of the guild's seasoned quilters to make such tiny, uniform stitches. She feared she would never be in a class with the creators of this lovely quilt. Tess imagined it displayed on a wall in the guest parlor of Iris House. But, no, she couldn't buy a raffle ticket. She didn't think it would look right if a guild member won the quilt. When she had time, she'd browse the other booths and perhaps find another quilt she liked as well for the Iris House parlor.

Meantime, she couldn't hold up this quilt much longer. Her arms were about to drop.

Tess blew a copper curl out of her eyes and sighed to herself. Then, "How about draping it over that chair," she suggested. Mary glanced at the high-backed oak rocker in the booth, then looked back at the quilt, her brow puckering.

Tess had come to know Mary only in the past few weeks, as they worked on the demonstration booth committee together, and she'd grown quite fond of her. They were both relative newcomers to town, Mary having lived in Victoria Springs for two years, only a few months longer than Tess. A widow, Mary had a fifteen-year-old daughter, Miranda, who was being excused from classes at the high school to help at the quilt show.

The high school home economics class had had a unit on quilting and had taken a booth to display the wall hangings made by the students. Miranda and a friend, Kendra Lawson, would be manning the home ec booth, which was next to the guild's booth, on one side. On the other side was The Quilter's Nook booth with displays of quilting supplies and fabrics offered for sale and projects done by students in the Nook's classes.

Tess waited as Mary Franks continued to ponder the placement of the Drunkard's Path quilt, her patience, like her arms, beginning to sag. She bit her tongue and reminded herself that Mary deserved an extra measure of forbearance. Tess's Aunt Dahlia, who somehow managed to uncover all the pertinent information about everybody in town without seeming to pry, had confided that Mary's husband had committed suicide and Mary had left Kansas City, where she'd lived all her life, to get away from the memories. A not uncommon reaction, Tess supposed. Unfortunately, unhappy memories could not be confined to a single location, and sometimes Mary's round blue eyes were so clouded with sadness that it made you want to gather her into your arms and weep.

The last few days, though, Mary's spirits had been uncharacteristically high because two of her oldest friends from Kansas City, Marlene Oxley and Cassie Terhune, would be in town. Tess had never seen Mary so energized. She'd seemed almost frenetic at times, but Tess thought that was better than being slumped in depression. It warmed Tess's heart to think that perhaps Mary was finally coming to grips with her husband's suicide.

Just as Tess was beginning to fear Mary had been struck dumb, Mary said, "No," rejecting Tess's suggestion for displaying the quilt with a shake of her head that made her short, tightly permed, brown ringlets bobble. Tess grimaced as her aching arms sagged even lower and she gathered the quilt to her chest.

"Oh, you poor thing," Mary said in a rush. "I've kept you holding that heavy quilt till your arms are about to fall off. I'm sorry, Tess."

Tess smiled wanly. "It's all right."

"It seems to me," Mary went on, "that the quilt will stand out more if we display it against the back wall of the booth."

"Good idea," Tess agreed. If Mary took as long to decide on the best place for every piece in the booth, they'd be there half the night. In fact, if Tess wasn't out of the exhibition hall in thirty minutes, she would have to cancel her dinner date, an eventuality she didn't even want to contemplate.

The two women took hold of either side of the quilt and lifted it above their heads to drape it over the top of the booth's back partition.

"By the way," Mary said, "can you handle raffle ticket sales tomorrow? I have to sell admission tickets at the door."

Tess thought about it. Her guests, all of whom were in town for the quilt show, should be out of the house by eight forty-five. Aunt Dahlia was coming at ten to help Tess work in the iris gardens surrounding Iris House, but they'd probably be ready for a break after a couple of hours of digging and replanting. "I could help in the afternoon," she said.

"Not all day?" Mary looked distracted and somehow helpless, which as usual made Tess want to accommodate her. Saying no to Mary, whatever the reason, made Tess feel selfish. "Oh, dear," Mary sighed. "I don't know who I'll get to stay in the booth tomorrow morning. Everybody on the committee already has an assignment."

Tess tried to stifle her resentment as her plans for Wednesday crumbled. It wasn't the end of the world. She'd just call Dahlia and put off working in the garden for another day. "I'll try to rearrange a few things and be here at nine then," she said.

Mary's blue eyes brightened and she looked relieved. "Oh, good." She smiled gratefully at Tess as she smoothed a wrinkle from the Drunkard's Path quilt.

As Tess turned to pick up another quilt, she saw Rex Brindle plowing through the hall as if the seat of his pants was on fire. She'd met Rex the previous evening when he arrived to take up occupancy in the Black Swan Room of Iris House. Rex was, Tess guessed, about thirty, of medium height, whipcord thin, and always seemed to crackle with nervous energy. His quick smile made Tess think of a mischievous child. At the moment, however, Rex wasn't smiling. And he looked more malevolent than mischievous. His brow, beneath the falling wings of black hair, was deeply furrowed, his mouth turned down at the corners, brown eyes slitted and boring straight ahead like lasers as he hurried for the exit.

Mary's brows rose quizzically as he sailed past the booth without a glance in their direction. "Rex," she called, "what's wrong?" If he heard, he gave no sign, but continued in a straight line for the door. Mary and Tess watched him grab the handle, throw the heavy door back as if he wanted to tear it off its hinges, and disappear into the gathering dusk.

Mary's mouth twisted wryly. "Dear me," she said. "Somebody must have rattled his cage."

Tess looked around the hall. "Who? Almost everybody is gone." She picked up a crib-sized quilt done in shades of blue and draped it over the back of the rocking chair, then reached for a fat teddy bear with a red ribbon around its neck from the box of props Mary had brought. She placed it in the chair with its head resting against the quilt.

Mary shrugged. "Could be anybody." She attached a small wall hanging to a booth partition with mounts that had adhesive on both sides. "He must have decided that somebody else got a better booth location than he did. In case you don't know, Rex has quite an ego."

"Have you known him long?"

"Oh, yes. He got into quilting while I lived in Kansas City. The first few shows he attended, he ran around preening and bragging about his work." Mary shook her head. "Honestly. We all thought he was a joke—until we got a look at his quilts. He's good, no doubt about that. And he doesn't mind telling you so. He gives the term 'tooting your own horn' new meaning."

From the little Tess had seen of him, she had to agree with Mary. Last night, as she showed him to his room, he'd made a point of telling her that one of his quilts had just sold for five figures and that he'd been invited to contribute three pieces for a show at the Metropolitan Museum of Art in New York City.

"He's not the most self-effacing person I ever met," Tess observed as she reached for another quilt. "But surely he knows the booths are assigned by drawing names."

"I expect he thinks he deserves special treatment."

Tess had no trouble believing that. "Could be," she murmured, looking around for a place to display the quilt she was holding. Noticing the quilt rack pushed to the back of the booth, she pulled it out and folded the quilt over one of its rungs. "Do you think we'll finish by seven?" she asked Mary. "I have a dinner engagement."

"You go on whenever you have to," Mary said. "If we aren't through, I'll finish up."

Grateful that Mary hadn't turned that helpless look on her again, Tess offered, "If you still think you'll need some of those two-by-fours upstairs, I'll help you bring them down before I leave."

Frowning, Mary looked up at the high, narrow loft that had been built as a storage area across the back of the exhibition hall. The loft was reached by way of metal stairs, which were fitted with rubber treads. The stairs were located against the east wall of the hall.

The two-by-fours Tess had referred to were eight feet long, and it would be difficult for one person to carry them down those narrow steps.

"I'm too tired to think about that right now," Mary said with a sigh. "If I see I need more boards, I'll get somebody to help me in the morning."

Hearing a sound, Tess glanced toward the front entrance and saw Shannon Diamond, one of her Iris House guests, open the door and take a step inside. Shannon scanned the hall quickly until her gaze came to rest on Mary Franks, who was still staring up at the lumber piled in the open loft.

After an instant of blank puzzlement, Shannon's eyes narrowed and her face twisted with what might have been hatred. Tess wasn't close enough to be sure, but Shannon's expression baffled her. Surely she had misread it.

Shannon glanced away from Mary and saw Tess. As

quickly as the rancorous expression had come, it disappeared and Shannon smiled brightly. "Yoo hoo!"

Mary, who hadn't noticed Shannon before, turned toward the source of the sound. The smile remained on Shannon's face as she approached, but Tess sensed that it was an effort for the young woman to keep it there. Had something happened at Iris House to upset Shannon? Tess worried. She could think of no other explanation for the quick change in Shannon's countenance from sunshine to shadow and back again. Certainly, Shannon couldn't be upset with Tess or Mary personally. As far as Tess knew, Shannon didn't know Mary, and she had met Tess less than twenty-four hours ago.

Shannon had arrived at Iris House at nine the previous night, and Tess had installed her in the Carnaby Room. Whenever possible, Tess assigned rooms according to her impression of her guests and had felt Shannon, finely attuned to colors because of her profession, would appreciate the strikingly sensuous roses, rubies, and pinks of the Carnaby Room. All the guest rooms in Iris House were named for irises. In addition to the Carnaby Room currently occupied by Shannon and the black, white, and yellow Black Swan Room assigned to Rex Brindle, there were the Annabel Jane Room, the Cliffs of Dover Room, the Arctic Fancy Room, and the Darcy Flame Suite, the only two-room accommodation in the house.

At breakfast that morning, Shannon had talked about her thriving interior decorating business; she seemed to be very successful for someone who was only in her mid-twenties. A pretty ash-blond with blue-green eyes, she had a way of looking at whomever she happened to be with at the moment that made you feel you were the most interesting person she'd met in ages. That focus may have helped account for her success.

"I thought that was you, Tess," Shannon said as she

reached the booth. She was wearing jeans and a crisp yellow knit shirt with white athletic shoes that looked new.

By contrast, Tess felt grungy. Wiping her hands down her rumpled, dust-smeared shirt and jeans, Tess shook off her worry that Shannon had come there to lodge a complaint against Iris House. She obviously had imagined that brief grimace, a trick of the light perhaps.

"Hi, Shannon." Tess tried to get on a first-name basis with her guests as quickly as possible. It contributed to the homey atmosphere she wanted to characterize her bed and breakfast. "I didn't expect to see you here. The show doesn't open until tomorrow."

"I know, but I came out for a walk, and when I saw the Civic Center, I decided to stop and see if I could get in and have a look around." She lowered her voice to a conspiratorial level. "I'm going to make a list of pieces I want to buy for my clients. Then I'll be here when the doors open tomorrow before the best items can be snatched up by somebody else." Shannon glanced at Mary, this time with a questioning smile and without a trace of dislike. There was more to this young woman than appeared on the surface, Tess mused. She thought her first take on Shannon's odd expression, as she caught sight of Mary from the doorway, had to be wrong. Unless Shannon had at first thought Mary was somebody else.

"Shannon, this is Mary Franks, president of our local quilters' guild. I think I told you at breakfast that I'd be helping Mary set up the guild's booth."

Mary, who was in the process of straightening a quilted cover on a small round table, turned and extended a hand as Shannon skirted the counter and entered the booth. "I'm pleased to meet you, Shannon. You mentioned clients. Do you own a quilt shop?"

"No, I'm an interior decorator. In Little Rock. I'm working with several people who go for the country look. It's still pretty big in Little Rock, though Southwestern decor and the lodge look are making inroads.''

''I would think quilts could be used with almost any decor,'' Mary said. ''They make a home so cozy and welcoming. They give any room a family feeling. Naturally, I love them since I'm such a family person.'' A shadow dulled Mary's eyes for a moment. She blinked it away.

Shannon was watching Mary in that intent way so characteristic of her, and Tess saw a look she couldn't identify cross Shannon's face, except that it was unpleasant. How strange. Could Shannon's thoughts actually be elsewhere while she appeared totally absorbed in what Mary was saying? Again, the inexplicable expression was gone in a flash and Shannon said to Mary, ''You're right. Quilts can enhance most any decor.''

''I have them all over my house,'' Mary said with a smile. ''I probably have too many of them on display, but I can't help it. Whenever I finish a new quilt, I just have to put it up somewhere.''

Shannon walked around the booth and began looking at the Drunkard's Path offerings, touching a wall hanging here, a quilt there. Mary returned to her work. After a moment, Shannon turned around as Mary held up a quilt by two corners. Mary glanced from the quilt she was holding to a side partition with half its breadth still unadorned.

''We'll put this one here.'' Mary laid the quilt aside and rummaged in a small box of nails on the counter. She picked out several and her gaze swept the counter. ''Drat! Where did I put that hammer?''

''Let me help you,'' Shannon offered. She looked under the rocker and the quilt rack. ''I don't see it.''

''I know I had it earlier today,'' Mary insisted, still staring at the counter, which was bare except for the box of nails and several quilt clamps. Finally, she turned and gazed around the booth with a perplexed frown. ''I need to hammer some nails to hold those big clamps. That quilt's heavy, it'll need at least three clamps.''

Tess sighed in exasperation. She was reluctant to leave, in spite of being short of time. Tess bent down to scan dark corners, but didn't see the hammer. Steadying herself with one hand against the partition where Mary intended to hang the next quilt, she started to straighten up when Mary cried in alarm, "Watch out, Tess." Tess froze. "Don't move," Mary ordered sharply. "Wait right there." Standing on tiptoe, she reached up and grabbed the hammer that was teetering on top of the partition. "There, I got it."

Tess stood and looked up at the narrow edge of the partition where the hammer had lain. Whoever had put it there had balanced it carefully. Hadn't they realized any movement of that partition would unbalance it and send it straight down?

Mary blanched as she ran a finger over the hammer's sharp claws. "Thank goodness I saw this in time. It would have fallen on you, Tess."

"That's a dangerous place to leave a hammer," Shannon put in.

"Did you leave it there, Tess?" Mary asked.

"No. I thought you might have."

Mary looked faintly insulted and shook her head. "I'm sure I left it on the counter the last time I used it."

"When was that?" Tess asked.

Mary thought for a moment. "Hours ago."

Tess recalled seeing the hammer on the counter at some point. But several people had been in and out of the booth during the day. Any one of them could have put the hammer on top of the partition. She tried to remember if she'd seen anyone pick it up from the counter, but she couldn't. She made an effort to shrug off an apprehensive feeling. After all, there'd been no harm done. Still, a niggling worry about her near-mishap with the hammer stayed with her.

Leaving the hammer on top of the partition was such a dangerous thing to do. Who could have been so thoughtless?

Pushing aside her anxiety, Tess glanced at her watch. "Mary, I hate to desert you. But I'm either going to have to leave now or call and cancel dinner."

Mary was still gazing at the hammer perplexedly. She glanced at Tess. "I can finish up. You go ahead."

Tess hesitated. "I hate to leave you alone here."

"I'll stay and help," Shannon offered quickly.

Mary darted a look at her, her expression one of blank surprise. "That's real sweet of you, but you came to look around, and you'd better hurry. The custodian will be locking up in less than an hour."

Shannon shrugged. "No big deal. I don't have to look around tonight. I can do it in the morning."

Shannon's offer of help seemed genuine, she wasn't just being polite. Tess studied the young woman's now-expressionless face. No big deal? That was a lightning-fast switch. Only a few moments ago, Shannon had seemed eager for the chance to get an early look at the merchandise.

Tess mulled it over, but could make no sense of the way Shannon was behaving. Undoubtedly there was an innocuous explanation.

Then why did she hesitate to leave the two women alone? She was just tired, she decided, and shook off her reluctance. She really couldn't wait to see if Mary accepted Shannon's offer of help. They were quite capable of settling it without her.

"I'll see both of you tomorrow," Tess said, rummaging for her purse beneath the counter. "Shannon, I hope you brought your key. The Iris House doors are locked by eight o'clock."

Shannon patted the hip pocket of her jeans. "Got it right here. See you tomorrow, Tess."

Tess grabbed her purse and left the hall, thinking it was uncommonly considerate of Shannon to delay touring the other booths in order to help a complete stranger. And no matter what she said, that *was* why she had stopped in the first place.

But perhaps Mary wasn't a stranger to Shannon. Tess still couldn't quite banish from her mind that look on Shannon's face as she had stared at Mary. Yet it had been obvious when Tess introduced them that Mary had never met Shannon before.

What with falling hammers, whatever the reason for Shannon's behavior, it was good that Mary would have company. Tess imagined the cavernous exhibition hall would seem downright spooky if you were alone there, after dark.

Chapter 3

Cassie Terhune was big-boned. It had been the rue of her existence as a teenager. Still was, truth be told. She certainly wasn't fat, though. She watched her weight carefully. When you were only five feet two inches tall, an extra five pounds showed. Yet, as closely as she watched her diet, Cassie's weight had always been near the top of the "normal" range on those insurance company charts. But what could you do about big bones? Why did so many of the women she knew have to be so slender, which translated to small-boned in Cassie's mind? Pure genetic luck, she thought enviously.

What she needed, Cassie thought wryly, was more chubby friends.

She pulled a slimming hip-length black tunic over her black stirrup pants, studying her mirrored reflection. The outfit made her look taller and thinner. She was an attractive woman, if not quite as tall and thin as the fantasy high-fashion-model image she carried of herself in her mind. Sometimes she put herself to sleep by dressing that image in various fashionable, figure-revealing outfits.

Her friend Marlene Oxley, with whom she was having dinner, was so skinny she looked good in almost anything, even horizontal stripes. Marlene didn't have a hip-length tunic to her name. For that matter, she hardly had any hips, Cassie thought maliciously. All Marlene's tops tucked in to show off her tiny waist. She rarely wore black, either, now that Cassie thought about it. Marlene could so easily have gone for the bright colors Cassie loved, but she seemed to prefer drab beiges and grays, as if she didn't want to call attention to herself. Marlene had always been a bit shy; she was a perfect match for her husband, Mike. The couple seemed to fade into the woodwork at any gathering.

Cassie sighed as she patted her dark, wavy hair into place. She gazed into her own gray eyes for a moment and turned her head to study her perfectly straight nose. At least, she thought, she was prettier than Marlene. And she looked years younger, too, even though Cassie was actually a year older than Marlene.

Everything evens out, she mused as she turned from the gilt-framed mirror in the Darcy Flame Suite. Then she remembered something her mother used to tell her and she laughed. *Cassie, you can't be best in everything. Nobody is.*

It was true that Cassie had always been competitive. She drove herself as hard now as she had when she'd held a high-pressure position as a corporate attorney. Not only did she want to be more successful and make more money than anybody else in her profession, she wanted to be skinnier than any of them, too. Ridiculous, Cassie chided herself, wishing she could feel more comfortable with herself, like plump Letitia Lattimore, who seemed never to give a thought to her figure. Or what she wore, for that matter. Cassie had seen Letitia in bold plaids and big-floral prints, neither of which did a thing for her. But then Letitia was nearly fifteen years older than Cassie. Perhaps acceptance of one's shortcomings grew with age.

Letitia could certainly use some help in her choice of quilt fabrics, and not just with her clothes. Cassie had offered magnanimously to help her choose more sophisticated color combinations for her quilts, but Letitia had bluntly declined. Whether or not Letitia had meant it as a put-down, Cassie had felt rebuked and irked by the feeling. She'd only been trying to help. She hadn't meant to insult Letitia. Honestly, you just couldn't help some people.

As for herself, Cassie mused, she did need to work on self-acceptance. By the time she was Letitia's age, she hoped she'd be free of her obsession with her weight and that inner voice that said she had to keep driving herself to greater achievements.

She moved from the bedroom, around the coral and blue Chinese folding screen that served as a divider, to 'the sitting room of the Darcy Flame Suite, and settled into an ivory Victorian slipper chair. It wasn't quite time yet to go downstairs and meet Marlene in the foyer.

Cassie had taken a booth in the Victoria Springs Quilt Show last year, staying in a hotel. But Iris House was more elegant, and a suite was more comfortable than a single room. This year, in addition to having a booth at the show, she'd been invited to conduct workshops. She'd agreed to three workshops only after the local quilt guild, the major sponsor of the show, had offered to enlist one of its members to oversee her booth during the workshops and to pay for her suite in ''one of Victoria Springs's newest and finest bed-and-breakfast inns.'' Iris House had opened its doors less than a year ago, she'd been told.

The suite was indeed fine, as promised, Cassie reflected, as her glance raked the quilted coral sofa, which was separated from two ivory, coral-ribbed Victorian slipper chairs by a low glass-topped table with heavy brass legs in the shape of giant S's. The suite was named for an iris, as were all the rooms in Iris House. The Darcy Flame, depicted in a gilt-framed oil painting that hung next to a swag-draped window, was a bright-coral hybrid iris. Tess Darcy had told Cassie, when she showed her to the suite, that the iris had been bred by Tess's late Aunt Iris, who had lived in the house until her death, when Tess had inherited it and turned it into a bed and breakfast.

And here Cassie was, in the only suite in the place which was being paid for by somebody else. Cream inevitably rose to the top, she told herself.

She couldn't help smiling when she remembered how Marlene had reacted when Cassie told her that her accommodations were being underwritten by the quilters' guild. Evidently Marlene, who would judge the quilts entered in the show, was paying for her own room. Although Marlene would never mention it, she would see Cassie's paid-for accommodations as a slap in the face, which somewhat made up for Marlene's incredible metabolism. Cassie was fully aware that she was being nasty. But it was OK to entertain petty thoughts, as long as you didn't voice them too often.

Sometimes, though, things slipped out. She couldn't seem to stop them. When she'd mentioned casually at breakfast that morning that the guild was picking up the tab for her suite, the look in Rex Brindle's eyes—a mixture of envy and dislike—had made her morning. Clearly Rex, who was conducting two workshops, was paying his own expenses. Cassie had felt a thrill of triumph as she tucked that realization away to gloat over in private.

Rex was such a cocky little rooster. He couldn't stand it that she was more successful than he. Oh, it was true that his quilts sold for more than hers, on the average. Only that morning, he'd made a point of telling her that he'd recently made a "very big" sale. He'd been dying to tell her exactly how much his precious creation had sold for, but she hadn't given him the chance. Cassie already thought he got preposterous prices for his contemporary quilts. One of a kind, they might be, but they were still only pieces of fabric sewn together, like every other quilt in existence.

Regardless, he didn't have his own TV show and publishing business. Publicly, Rex said he wouldn't dream of diffusing his artistic imagination by polluting it with thoughts of mere business enterprise, but in his spiteful little heart, Cassie was sure, jealousy roiled like a stormy sea. What Rex couldn't get was that they weren't in art as much as they were in business. Her background in corporate law, as stressful as it had been and as badly as it had ended, had stood her in good stead in her present profession. She could teach Rex a thing or two were she so inclined—but, of course, he wouldn't accept help from her in any case.

Cassie enjoyed indulging in secret malicious delight at Rex's expense, but she wouldn't want to cross him openly. Rex would find a way to get even. He was that kind of person.

The thought sent a little frisson of unease through Cassie. Her new book contained one or two quilt patterns that were variations of drawings she'd seen in Rex's office when she took some of her students to tour his studio. Not that she'd done anything illegal, and she'd been up against a deadline. After all, his drawings were little more than doodling. The patterns hadn't been finished yet, and for all she knew Rex could have discarded every one of them. Besides, she told herself, she'd changed them enough so that he would never recognize them.

She brushed aside her anxiety and glanced at her watch. It was time to go downstairs. She was glad to be getting out among people, even though she didn't expect to enjoy dinner all that much. Marlene was a loyal friend, but not a great conversationalist. They'd invited Mary Franks to join them for dinner, but Mary was involved in setting up her quilting guild's booth. Which was just as well, Cassie had thought when she'd heard it. Mary was no fun anymore. She'd been moping around for two years, ever since her husband committed suicide. It was a tragedy, of course, but it was time Mary stopped brooding on it.

Even though she'd long ago lost patience with Mary's self-pity, when Mary had invited Cassie and Marlene to dinner at her house Wednesday evening, Cassie had felt obliged to accept. She heaved a martyr's sigh. Good Lord, two years was more than enough time for Mary to have put that unpleasantness behind her and get on with her life. If Mary brought it up at dinner tomorrow, Cassie was really going to have to work not to appear unsympathetic.

Being unsympathetic about other people's pain had been one of several things her ex-husband had accused her of when he left her. He'd also said she was the most selfish person he'd ever known and had no character. Or empathy, don't forget that one.

But nobody knew about that. Cassie had told everyone that she'd dumped Ralph. She'd acted as though she was vastly relieved to be out of the marriage.

She'd die of humiliation if any of her friends knew the truth.

She pulled on a long-lined black and white checked cardigan over her tunic and left the room.

After leaving the exhibition hall, Rex Brindle had found the steak house and had dinner alone to give himself time to cool off before confronting Cassie. He had finally succeeded in getting a rein on his fiery temper. Eventually his hot rage had turned to an icy desire for revenge. He returned to Iris House and stepped into the foyer just as Cassie descended the stairs.

"Good evening, Rex," she greeted him. "Finally got your booth arranged to your liking?"

Rex halted in his tracks. Just look at her, he thought.

Bold as brass. Some of the fire he'd thought tamped down flared up. Chest heaving, Rex said, "Yes, and I had a look at your booth, too." His words were like bullets cracking from his mouth, one after the other in rapid succession.

She tilted her head to look up at him curiously. The picture of perfect innocence. God, he wanted to kill her!

"I just threw it together, really. I'm sure my booth isn't as attractive as yours, but then I'm afraid I'm not as particular about all the little details as you are."

"Perhaps you should be."

She hesitated, as though the tension in him bewildered her. What an actress! "Rex, are you all right? You look pale. Are you sick? Nauseated?"

"I'm getting there, Cassie. If you keep up this act much longer, I may just puke all over you."

"What—?"

He overrode her. "You literally make me sick, Cassie!"

"Well!" she huffed.

Again, he spoke before she could continue. "I always knew you had no ethics, but have you no pride, either?"

Though she was trying to pretend indifference, he was clearly getting to her. She thrust out her jaw. "I'm going to overlook that insult, Rex. Obviously you're not yourself."

"Oh, that's rich!"

Her gray eyes flashed. "Have you been drinking?"

"No, I have not. But I did have the misfortune to glance through your new book this evening. That's why I'm 'not myself,' as if you haven't already guessed."

She stiffened. "What *are* you raving about?"

"You've gone too far this time, Cassie."

"No, *you've* gone too far! You've slipped a cog, Rex," she snapped. Her voice held irritation, but still no hint of concern or apology. She moved as if to walk past him.

He felt a muscle flicker in his jaw and his hands tightened into fists at his sides as he blocked her way. "You're nothing but a common thief! You can't design anything original yourself, so you stole four of my designs."

Her lips drew back in a parody of a smile. "Oh, really, Rex. Pray tell me how on earth I did that. You're always so secretive about your precious designs."

"You did it when you were in my studio last year. I wondered at the time why you'd come. Now I know."

She widened her eyes so that white showed all around. Then she threw back her head and laughed, exposing a smooth, ivory throat that his hands itched to squeeze. "How ridiculous," she said. "As I recall, I was feeling unwell, too sick to think about anybody's designs. You really should see a counselor about that paranoia of yours, Rex."

He took a step toward her. It was all he could do not to slap that sly smile off her face. "You stole my designs!"

Her face stiffened into a mask of contempt. "Prove it."

"I intend to. I'm seeing a lawyer. I'm prepared to do whatever it takes to expose you for the thief you are, Cassie Terhune!"

Her gray eyes had turned as hard as steel. "I advise you, Rex, don't make threats you can't back up," she said grimly. "And be careful what you say. I won't hesitate to charge you with slander. Now step aside and let me pass."

Rex was losing his grip on his fury. What might have happened next, he was never to know, for at that moment, the front door burst open and a handsome, blond man stepped into the tension-filled foyer.

The newcomer was in his early thirties, tall and lean with eyes as blue as a summer sky over the open prairie on the clearest day of the year. Women must flock after him, Cassie thought. She had an impulse to hug him, which she repressed. She was so grateful for his appearance at such a critical moment.

The man hesitated, looking from Rex's face to Cassie's. It was obvious that he realized he'd walked into the middle of a conflict. "Excuse me," he said formally. "I've come to pick up Tess."

Lucky Tess, Cassie thought, her eyes lingering on the young man's back.

As he knocked on Tess's apartment door, Marlene Oxley came down the stairs in a drab beige pantsuit. "Thank goodness," Cassie greeted her. "Let's get out of here." She grabbed Marlene's arm and hustled her out the door.

"What happened? What's wrong?" Marlene asked, practically running to keep up with Cassie.

"It's nothing."

"But Rex—"

"Forget it!" Cassie snapped. "Rex is just in one of his snits."

Rex was left standing alone in the foyer, his rage unabated.

Chapter 4

Tess was so glad that she hadn't had to cancel her dinner date with Luke, who'd been out of town on business since Friday. In spite of her resolution not to get involved with a man until her bed and breakfast was well established, she'd met Luke Fredrik while the Darcy family's old Victorian house, Tess's inheritance from her Aunt Iris, was being renovated. As chairman of the Chamber of Commerce board, Luke had come to Iris House, while it was still being transformed, to welcome her to town and offer the chamber's services. She'd been grimy and bedraggled from stripping layers of varnish off the oak roll-top desk that had come with the house. Luke, on the other hand, had looked like a model for *GQ* in a dark business suit. Mortified by her appearance, she'd stammered thanks for his call. When he left, she'd allowed herself a moment to regret that such a perfect specimen of the male sex would undoubtedly never think of her again.

When he had called a couple of weeks later to ask her out, she'd surprised herself by accepting. With the months-long renovation and then the opening of Iris House, she truly hadn't had time for romance that first year, but Luke had found ways for them to be

together, stolen hours sandwiched between her loving su-
pervision of Iris House and his business as portfolio manager and investment adviser to two dozen hand-picked
clients.

After more than a year of seeing Luke, Tess felt ridic-
ulously abandoned when he had to be out of town. Not that
they were together every day or even every evening, but
when he was in town, she knew she *could* see him if she
felt the need. And no matter how many times she denied it
to herself, Luke had slowly but surely become a need in
her life.

Alas, she was very much afraid she was in love with
Luke, although she'd never told him so. He had had no
such reluctance and, lately, he'd obliquely broached the
subject of marriage a couple of times. Marriage was
something Tess did not even want to think about for a long
while. Would Luke expect her to move into his big house,
where he was connected to Wall Street by computer, mo-
dem, and fax machine? Since he lived alone, the lovely old
house inherited from his parents provided ample room for
his offices as well as living quarters.

One of the things she liked most about running Iris
House was that she had her own adored apartment on the
premises, which she shared with Primrose, an uppity gray
Persian left to her by her late Aunt Iris.

Tess had lovingly planned every detail of the apartment's
decor, and leaving it would be like leaving a doted-on child.
Besides, if she ever moved in with Luke, Primrose would
have to go, too, and she could not imagine Primrose con-
senting to such an arrangement. Nor could she imagine
Luke moving into her lovely, but not large, apartment. He
needed a good-sized office, for one thing, and room to entertain clients, for another.

It was all too troublesome to think about. Tess liked
things just the way they were. She would be thirty next

summer; there was plenty of time for marriage plans in the vague future. Fortunately, Luke was the most laid back person Tess knew. His philosophy was to relax and let things work themselves out. Sitting in the quiet, dimly lighted restaurant with Luke seated across the table from her in a heather-gray crew-necked sweater, his head in the menu, she took the opportunity to admire the way the soft light from a nearby wall fixture highlighted his chiseled features and made his hair gleam like spun gold.

He looked up and, snagging her glance with his blue eyes, reached across the small table to caress her cheek. She'd often read in novels about someone's heart turning over, but she'd never experienced it before Luke. The way he was looking at her made her glad she'd worn her yellow and green silk dress, her best colors with her auburn curls and brown eyes.

"Did you miss me, love?" he inquired softly.

Obviously it was a rhetorical question, for there was no shadow of doubt on his handsome face. "Yes," she admitted with a rueful smile. Lest he become too sure of himself, she amended hastily, "Of course, I was very busy with preparations for the quilt show."

His eyes twinkled. "And welcoming a whole new group of house guests?"

"Uh-huh. They're all involved in quilting, one way or another. I never realized before how many people are."

Their waiter appeared and took their orders, poached salmon and brown rice for Luke, charcoal-grilled filet mignon and a vegetable medley for Tess.

As the waiter departed, Luke poured two glasses of wine from the bottle he'd ordered earlier. "Speaking of your house guests—" As he lifted his goblet, prisms of light danced in the crystal bowl, as if it were suddenly, magically filled with diamonds. But the magical illusion was shattered by his next words. "Two of them were in the foyer when

I arrived at Iris House. I had the distinct impression they'd been quarreling.''

Tess nodded unhappily. "That was Rex Brindle and Cassie Terhune. Both are well-known as master quilters. I recognized their voices, but I heard only scraps of what they were saying, though enough to know it was definitely unpleasant. In fact, I heard Rex accuse Cassie of stealing some of his quilt designs."

Luke's brows rose in amusement. "That sweet-looking little thing?"

For some reason, Luke's description of Cassie Terhune rankled. "I don't think she's as sweet as she seems. Sometimes when she doesn't know you're observing her, she gets this look—calculating is the best word I can think of to describe it."

"Mmm-hmm," murmured Luke noncommittally.

"She puts people down, too."

"You've heard her?"

"Absolutely. This afternoon, she and Letitia Lattimore were in the guest parlor." At Luke's puzzled expression, Tess inserted, "Letitia's another quilter, and a nice lady besides. She's in the Arctic Fancy Room."

"Ah," was Luke's only comment.

"Anyway, Letitia was talking excitedly about a quilt she'd just finished, saying how well it had turned out. She was so pleased with it. Then Cassie, in this snide voice, said something about it being another 'sweet pink and blue creation,' which apparently are Letitia's favorite colors. It was obvious Cassie meant it as an insult, Luke."

"What's wrong with pink and blue?" Luke inquired.

"According to Cassie, the combination is unsophisticated. She had the unmitigated nerve to offer to help Letitia pick classier color combinations. Letitia thanked her politely, but didn't take her up on it."

"Sounds like a tempest in a teapot."

Tess was sure Cassie and Letitia didn't view it in that light. "Back to Rex's accusation," she went on, "it's a serious one, Luke. Most quilters are just"—she gestured helplessly—"well, *quilters*. They buy patterns and fabric off the bolt and use them in their own quilts. Many times they use the colors shown on the pattern envelope or duplicate quilts they've seen in quilt magazines. But Rex and Cassie are *quilt artists*. They create the quilts shown in magazines. Rex is known particularly for his original designs. And Cassie has her own TV show and publishing business. I think *that* has ruffled some feathers, too."

Luke was looking a bit lost. "What has?"

"Cassie's venture into publishing."

"Sounds like smart business. Who could object to that?"

"Cassie created a separate company to publish her own books," Tess explained, "and, from something Marlene Oxley—another of my guests—said, there are hard feelings between Cassie and Julian and Phyllis Hyde, who publish quilting books and a magazine. The Hydes wanted to publish Cassie's books, but she demanded such a large advance and so much control that it wasn't financially feasible. So Cassie just formed her own publishing company. According to Marlene, she's also thinking about starting a magazine to compete with the Hydes'."

"Let me get this straight. You say this Oxley woman is staying with you. Are the Hydes at Iris House as well?"

"Yes, didn't I mention that?"

"No, you didn't." He cocked his head and gave her a mystified smile. "Tell me, honey, how do you always manage to fill your house with people who dislike each other?"

Tess shrugged. "I certainly don't plan it. It just happens, Luke."

Luke sipped his wine reflectively. "Let's get back to Brindle versus Terhune. What did Ms. Terhune have to say to Mr. Brindle's charges?"

"She denied everything. She even laughed at him and said he was paranoid. And then she threatened to sue him for slander."

A blond brow shot up. "I thought you only heard scraps of their conversation."

"Quite a few of them, actually," she responded, ignoring the humor in his eyes. "I don't think Rex tolerated Cassie's attitude at all well. He takes his work, and himself, very seriously."

Luke lifted both brows this time. "It appears that people will fight to protect their turf, no matter what business they're in."

Frowning, Tess took a drink of wine. Luke didn't seem to realize that for the people who made their living from quilting, it wasn't a hobby. It was serious business. "I just hope Rex doesn't make another scene in front of my other guests."

"Don't worry about it," Luke said offhandedly. "If he does, nobody can blame you."

"Luke, you know I feel responsible for creating a pleasant atmosphere for my guests," she protested.

He set down his goblet and took her hand in both of his. "Don't fret, sweetheart."

Oh, right. Go with the flow. That was Luke's outlook. In all fairness, it worked admirably for him. Somehow, in his high-pressure business, he managed to ride the waves serenely. Tess, on the other hand, was a worrier, particularly where Iris House was concerned.

"Let's change the subject," Luke suggested. "You said you were going to help set up the quilt guild's booth for the show. How did that go?"

Tess's frown eased away. "It'll be one of the most attractive booths in the hall, if I do say so myself. Of course, Mary Franks deserves most of the credit. Every piece had to be placed exactly right. She was still working in the booth when I left to get ready for dinner."

"It's probably good for her to keep busy," Luke observed. "The last time you mentioned her, you said she still looked sad all the time."

Tess nodded. "I know it's been two years since her husband died, but it's not that long when you consider that she's not just trying to get over his death. The man *chose* to die. She can't seem to put that behind her. She's perked up this week, though. For one thing, two of her oldest friends are in town for the quilt show. In fact, Cassie Terhune is one of them. Mary told me she's known Cassie for almost twenty years—Cassie left the practice of law to get into quilting, by the way—and Mary and Marlene Oxley went to high school together." Tess's hand was still in Luke's. She laced her fingers through his, returning the pressure of his strong, warm hand.

He looked at her inquiringly. "It'll be good for Mary to be with her old friends. Maybe she can forget about her husband for a few days."

"I hope so." Tess puckered her brow in thought. "What on earth would make a man with a loving wife and daughter kill himself? Do you suppose he had a fatal disease that he hadn't told anybody about?"

Luke studied her for a moment before he responded. "I wouldn't want what I'm about to say to get around, for Mary's sake."

Tess nodded solemnly.

"Gerald Franks was under federal indictment for insider trading. If he hadn't died, he'd have gone to prison."

Stunned, Tess stared at him. "Mary's husband? How do you know this, Luke?"

He lifted his shoulders. "Franks was an account executive at one of the biggest brokerage houses in Kansas City. I have a couple of friends who work there. Besides, it was all over the Kansas City papers."

"No wonder Mary moved away," Tess murmured. "Oh, that poor woman. And poor little Miranda." Miranda had been only thirteen when she and Mary moved to Victoria Springs. "But maybe Miranda doesn't know. That could be one of the reasons Mary left Kansas City, to keep her daughter from ever learning the truth about her father."

"Hmm, could be."

Tess eyed Luke quizzically. Sometimes, when he talked about the world of high finance and investing, she felt at sea without a rudder. "Exactly what is insider trading?"

He released her hand and settled back in his chair. "Making use of inside information to make money in the stock market," he summarized succinctly. "An international conglomerate wanted to buy Hexler Corporation, a Kansas City–based company—they design computer software used by some of the biggest businesses in the country. They'd been bargaining back and forth over the purchase price of the company's stock for months, and the offering price kept going up. All very hush-hush, of course, so the company's stock remained at more than ten dollars per share below the conglomerate's offer. Franks got wind of the deal somehow. It was surmised that one of his clients, who was an officer at Hexler, told him the news in confidence. To the end, he refused to name his source. Anyway, shortly before the pending purchase was made public, which caused the stock to shoot up twelve points per share—that's dollars to you, love—Franks borrowed big bucks and bought options to buy the stock at the then market price. After the price soared, he exercised his options and resold the stock."

"An option means you can buy or sell a stock at a certain price for a certain period of time, right?" Luke had explained options and futures to her before.

"Very good, dear heart. You remember your lessons well. And since options cost much less than the stock itself, you can have control of many more shares of stock than if you'd bought the shares outright.''

"It sounds just like gambling to me," Tess observed. She had never understood Luke's fascination with the stock market. It seemed frighteningly unpredictable.

"In some cases, it is. In Franks's case, though, it was a sure thing, and he might have gotten away with it, but he made the mistake of also buying options for some of his biggest clients. The vastly increased activity in the stock prior to the announced buyout caused such a glitch in the SEC's computers that they began investigating Franks.''

"The Securities and Exchange Commission?'' Tess queried. Luke nodded. Tess chewed her lip thoughtfully. "But how could they know it wasn't just a lucky guess on Franks's part? Can't anybody buy stocks or options in any company they want?''

Luke chuckled. "Not if they have access to inside information. It's illegal, sweet.''

"But how could anybody prove Franks had access when he bought the options?''

"That many options? Franks himself made a million and a half on the deal. His clients, a total of another couple million. Franks claimed it was just a lucky educated guess, but apparently that was simply too much for the SEC to swallow. Besides, you can be sure their investigation turned up some hard evidence or they'd never have charged Franks.''

"But the clients had no knowledge of what Franks knew, did they?''

"Not as far as I know. Evidently they trusted his judgment enough to buy the options upon his recommendation.''

"Did they all have to give back the money?''

"They reached an agreement with the SEC. It was never made public, but my guess is it was a compromise. They probably gave up a percentage of their profits, even though they'd had no inside information.''

What a disappointment that must have been! ''Do you ever recommend options to your clients, Luke?''

He shook his head. ''I tend toward financial conservatism when I'm advising other people on how to spend their money. I've taken a flyer myself once or twice, but I don't make a habit of it.''

Tess sighed. ''I'm glad you're the one in the investment business. I have enough problems running a bed and breakfast.'' She rolled her shoulders to ease the tight ache between her shoulder blades. ''Oh, what a day.''

''Tired?''

''A little.''

''When are we going to get out of town together for a few days? We could both use the R and R.''

It wasn't the first time Luke had mentioned it, and the idea was truly tempting. But several problems presented themselves to Tess's mind. For one thing, sharing a vacation seemed a statement of a deeper commitment than she was willing to make at present. It was too much like a honeymoon. Luke might not agree with her, but it bothered her nevertheless. And she wasn't sure she could voice her reservations without hurting him. Why couldn't he understand that things were perfect as they were?

There was another problem, too. ''I can't even think about leaving town until the tourist season is over,'' she said. That would be mid-December. ''And then there's Christmas. I don't know yet what my father's plans are for the holidays.''

Tess's father, stepmother, and their two children lived in France, where her father was assigned to the diplomatic corps at the American embassy.

''I think you could leave Iris House in someone else's hands for a couple of days—but I gather this isn't a good time to talk about vacations," Luke observed. "You're too tired."

Tess was grateful he wasn't going to pursue the subject. She sighed. "Helping Mary in the booth gave me a workout. I used muscles I haven't used in months." She had intended for some time to start a fitness program. Walking, perhaps, or biking. But somehow there never seemed to be time in her schedule for exercise, no more than for quilting.

Luke grinned devilishly, wriggled his eyebrows, and said in his W. C. Fields voice, "When we get back to your place, I'll give you a nice, relaxing back massage, my little chickadee."

Tess laughed. "I'll take you up on that. And maybe tomorrow night I'll get you to massage my feet. I'll probably be on them all day. I agreed to sell raffle tickets in the guild's booth."

"Sounds to me as though you're doing more than your share of the guild's work."

"Can't blame that on anybody but myself. I volunteered."

"Tell you what. I could spell you for an hour tomorrow afternoon, if you'd like. I need to put in an appearance at the show sometime. The Chamber of Commerce is a co-sponsor, you know." Luke was still chairman of the local chamber's board of directors.

"That would be wonderful, Luke. It'll give me a chance to sit down for a while and have a cup of coffee. I really hadn't planned to spend all day at the show, but Mary needed somebody and, well"—she sighed again—"what can I say? I felt sorry for her and agreed to do it. Aunt Dahlia was coming to help me in the iris gardens tomorrow morning, but I was able to reschedule that for Thursday."

Their waiter approached, bearing their dinner on a big brass tray. As the waiter served them, Tess inhaled the invigorating smell of good food expertly prepared. Tess's vegetable medley consisted of bright, crisp broccoli spears and carrot circles. Her steak was thick and oozed juice when she cut off a bite-sized piece. "Umm, this looks delicious." The waiter bowed his thanks and departed. Tess picked up the piece of steak with her fork. "I just now realized how hungry I am." Gazing into Luke's eyes, she felt a warm surge of delight. A beautiful October evening in the Ozarks. A delicious dinner in a romantic setting with the best man imaginable. What more could a woman ask for? She tasted the filet and luxuriated in the perfect mingling of a subtle dash of garlic and prime beef cooked over charcoal.

"Tess, love." Luke was looking quite serious all of a sudden. "You don't think you're taking on too much, with the garden club and the quilt show and Iris House?"

Dear Luke. Although he hadn't said it left too little time for the two of them to be together, she was sure he was thinking it. Tess swallowed and said stalwartly, "I've missed the last two garden club meetings, and, after tomorrow, I'll let other guild members take over the booth. Nobody will be able to say I shirked. Besides, I'm feeling refreshed already. I'll be good as new after this dinner and a good night's sleep."

"Sleep?" Luke inquired lazily.

A grin tugged at the corners of her mouth. "Well, there may be a few other things on my schedule first."

"Like your massage and, uh . . ." He left the sentence dangling, but he didn't need the words. His meaning was in his eyes.

Tess felt her cheeks flush. "Uh? You're usually so articulate, Luke."

He chuckled. "There are times when words fail me."

"Just as well, too." Gazing into his handsome face, she asked herself how she had ever been lucky enough to meet this delightful man. She cleared her throat and asked briskly, "You won't forget about taking over the guild's booth for a while tomorrow?"

"Not a chance."

"Good. What time do you think you can be at the Civic Center?"

"Let me see how my morning goes first."

Chapter 5

The next morning, Tess and Gertie Bogart, the Iris House cook, drove to the Civic Center in Tess's car. Gertie's church was running the concession stand at the quilt show as a fund-raiser for the missionary society. Gertie was in charge of desserts. She'd given herself the assignment for today; her contributions were in a box on her lap. Brownie Muffins and Scrumptious Chocolate Chip Cookies, both of which she had prepared several times for the Sunday afternoon teas in the Iris House library. Gertie was generally acknowledged to be the best cook in town. Recently, she'd begun compiling some of her recipes for a cook book. Like many fine cooks, Gertie sometimes overindulged in her own good cooking. Consequently, she was thirty pounds overweight, and she dressed for comfort in a variety of floral print tent dresses.

Even though Tess had enjoyed a filling breakfast of Gertie's Cherry-Cream Crepes and Canadian bacon, the odors wafting from Gertie's box made her mouth water.

"Would it be too self-serving of me to buy a dozen of your muffins?" Tess asked.

Gertie chuckled. "No need. I saved you some.

They're back at Iris House in the cabinet next to the refrigerator.''

"Thank you, Gertie. You know how much I love those muffins."

"Almost as much as Luke loves them, I'd say," Gertie responded. Her round face with its splurge of pale freckles softened, as it always did when she spoke of Luke. Gertie considered him the best catch in Victoria Springs and extolled the virtues of marriage to a good man whenever Tess would sit still long enough to listen. Clearly, Gertie feared that Tess would dally so long that Luke would be snatched away by a wiser woman who recognized perfect husband material when she met it.

Glancing at Gertie, Tess suppressed a smile. In one of her loose tent dresses, this one splashed with yellow daffodils, with her short, sandy hair held in place by a yellow headband, Gertie carried the box in her ample lap, gripping the edges firmly.

"I'll share them with Luke," Tess promised.

"Such a fine young man," Gertie murmured, but loudly enough for Tess to hear.

"Uh-huh," Tess responded as she turned into the Civic Center parking lot. "Oh, look. There's Shannon Diamond. She wasn't kidding when she said she'd be here when the doors opened."

As they got out of Tess's car, they watched Shannon, in a soft blue shirtwaist dress, disappear into the exhibition hall. "Seems like a right friendly girl," Gertie mused, but her face creased in thought.

"Here, let me carry that for a while," Tess said, taking the big box of goodies from Gertie's hands.

They walked slowly toward the hall, enjoying the mild October day. The hazy Indian summer sky turned the surrounding mountains a muted purple that shimmered into blue where mountain met sky. Tess inhaled the crisp smell of fall while her eyes drank in the deep orange and red foliage of the oak trees lining Hill Street, which ran in front of the Civic Center as well as the post office, police station and city hall south of the center. The leaves were so richly hued they appeared, at first glance, to be on fire. Since she'd moved to Victoria Springs, fall was Tess's favorite season. The beauty of an Ozark autumn was enough to take your breath away.

"Asks an awful lot of strange questions, though," Gertie mumbled.

Tess drew her admiring gaze from the oak trees, returning her attention to Gertie. "Who?"

"Shannon Diamond."

"Really?"

Gertie nodded. "She came down to the kitchen a half-hour before breakfast this morning. Got herself a cup of coffee, and sat down at the kitchen table to drink it."

"And ask strange questions?" Tess prompted.

"Well . . ." Gertie paused thoughtfully. "Not *strange*, exactly, but it seemed a bit odd that she was so interested in strangers. I finally decided she knew Mary Franks from somewhere else, but when I asked her about it, she said she met her only last night. Then she went right on with her questions."

"She questioned you about Mary?"

"She sure did. Wanted to know how long Mary had lived in Victoria Springs, where she'd lived before that, what was Mary's daughter like, did they have any relatives here. She even wanted to know about Mary's late husband. I told her I'd never heard Mary say much about him and, as for me, I never set eyes on the man." She glanced at Tess and gave a perplexed shake of her head. "Wanted to know what he'd looked like, as if I had any earthly idea."

Tess's face scrunched in reflection. "That *is* odd." In the middle of the parking lot, she shifted the box of baked goods off the spot where a corner was digging into her arm through the sleeve of her rust-colored cotton sweater. "Shannon stayed to help Mary with the guild's booth last night, after I left. Sounds like Mary really piqued Shannon's curiosity."

Even as she spoke the words, they didn't ring true to Tess. Mary was not the sort of person one would describe as "fascinating" or "intriguing" or even, to be honest, "interesting." Mary was pleasant and sad, but not terribly mysterious. Furthermore, Tess still hadn't banished from memory the expression that came over Shannon's face last evening, when she stepped into the exhibition hall and caught sight of Mary. Tess's eyes narrowed in concentration. What was going on in Shannon Diamond's pretty blond head? Tess couldn't shake the feeling that it was something devious.

They reached the exhibition hall and Gertie held the door open for Tess to pass through with the box. The concession stand was directly ahead, in the open area separating two cavernous rooms, one of which would accommodate the quilt show booths for the next several days. Tess slid the box onto the counter of the concession stand and greeted the two women who were chopping onions and slicing tomatoes for hamburgers. "Save me one of those chocolate chip cookies to go with my lunch burger, Gertie," Tess said. "I'm not sure what time I'll eat. I have to wait until Luke, or somebody, can relieve me at the guild's booth."

Gertie brightened at the mention of Luke, but before she could think of another flattering observation about that "fine young man," Tess excused herself.

Mary Franks sat at a small table near the open doorway leading to the quilt show, a roll of tickets and a cash box in front of her. Her worried frown eased when she saw Tess, who glanced at her watch and realized that it was five minutes after nine.

"Sorry to be late," Tess apologized. "Had any customers yet?"

"Only a few, but I just spotted a big tour bus pulling into the parking lot. I told Miranda to keep an eye on the guild booth till you got here, in case anybody wanted to buy a raffle ticket."

Tess hesitated, wanting to ask Mary about how she and Shannon Diamond had hit it off last evening, after Tess left. But two women were approaching the table, and Tess said instead, "I'd better get to work. See you later, Mary."

Tess paused at The Quilter's Nook booth to say hello to the owner, Sandra Patterson, a fiftyish woman with rosy cheeks and a sweet smile. Sandra was dressed for comfort in jeans and a pink T-shirt decorated with The Quilter's Nook logo, a nine-patch block with a threaded needle stuck in it. Placing a hand on the booth counter, Tess almost knocked over a basket filled with quilters' rotary cutters.

Reacting quickly, Sandra grabbed the basket. "Oops. I'd better set this back a ways." Designed to cut through several layers of fabric at one time, the rotary cutters had circular roller blades that were as sharp as razors. "So, what are you doing here so early, Tess?"

"I'm in charge of the quilt guild's booth today."

"Maybe we can have a cup of coffee together some time during the morning."

Tess said that she didn't know when she would be able to get away and moved to the home ec display, on the other side of the Drunkard's Path booth, to speak to Miranda Franks and Kendra Lawson. The two fifteen-year-olds wore jeans and long-sleeved red T-shirts decorated with VSHS in large black letters above a black bear's head, for the high school football team, the Victoria Springs Bears. Behind them, the booth walls were covered with small, colorful, pieced and quilted wall hangings. Most of them were made from the Ohio Star pattern, though Tess saw a few Log

Cabin and Tumbling Blocks variations. About half of the wall hangings had price tags of twenty or twenty-five dollars attached. Evidently, the unpriced hangings belonged to students who wanted to keep their handiwork.

Shannon Diamond, her eyes as true a blue as Tess had ever seen them, because of Shannon's blue dress, was leaning against the counter, talking to the girls. It was beginning to look as though wherever Mary or Miranda Franks might happen to be, Shannon Diamond could be found close by.

"Good morning," Tess said.

Shannon straightened up. "Oh, hi, Tess." After a glimmer of irritation crossed her face, she flashed Tess a smile. "I was just getting acquainted with Miranda and Kendra. But I'd better make my rounds now." She lifted her hand in a wave as she left the booth. "See you all later."

Tess watched her go before turning to Miranda. "Shannon's staying at Iris House."

Miranda raked a strand of long, curly dark blond hair out of her hazel eyes and shrugged. "Yeah, she told us. She's sure friendly. She said my mother talked about me last night, when Shannon was helping her with the Drunkard's Path booth, and she wanted to meet me."

"She's like really nice," Kendra chimed in, popping her gum. A smile wrinkled her short, round nose. Her brown bangs covered her eyebrows, making Tess's fingers itch to take a pair of scissors to them. The rest of Kendra's hair was pulled back in a single braid with a red ribbon tied near the end.

"Yeah," Miranda agreed. "I'm like, Who me? when she asked us to have lunch with her. I mean, we just met her and she's like twenty-four or -five, at least."

Practically decrepit, Tess thought from her own ancient perspective of going-on-thirty years. "It does seem—well, unusual, her inviting two girls she doesn't know to lunch."

Kendra nodded enthusiastically and plucked at her bangs.

"She's *real* easy to talk to. You almost forget she's so much older. She even said we could pick the restaurant."

"I think we should pick the Sampler Tea Room," Miranda said to Kendra.

"We just *love* the Sampler Tea Room," Kendra told Tess.

"We think it has *atmosphere*," Miranda said gravely.

"And like *class*," Kendra added.

The tea room, a converted Victorian house not far from Iris House, was a popular lunch place for tourists and residents alike. The menu offered a variety of wonderful salads, among other things, in a cozy, relaxed setting. Compared to the high school cafeteria, Tess guessed the tea room *could* be described as atmospheric and classy.

Leaving aside thoughts of the tea room, Tess returned to the nagging little worry about Shannon's motives. "You will clear it with your mother before having lunch with Shannon, won't you, Miranda?" she asked.

Miranda looked blank. "Well, sure. But she won't care. Why should she?"

Tess didn't know, but there was something decidedly fishy in Shannon Diamond's uncommon interest in Mary Franks and her daughter. Was it possible that they were the real reason Shannon was in Victoria Springs, and buying items for her clients was just a convenient cover? But why? Tess could think of no rational explanation.

Which left irrational ones. For example, if Shannon was a psycho who fixated on strangers for her own insane reasons . . . Tess almost laughed aloud as that wild idea crossed her mind. As unusual as her interest in Mary and Miranda was, Shannon had given no indication of being neurotic, much less crazy.

Don't let your imagination dash off in outlandish directions, Tess cautioned herself.

A noisy group of elderly people, mostly female, entered

the exhibition hall. They must have come in on that tour bus Mary had seen. Tess scooted back to the Drunkard's Path booth as several of them stopped to read the sign about the raffle. She did a brisk business in raffle tickets after that. During the lulls, she was able to locate all of her guests in the hall.

Julian and Phyllis Hyde, who were staying in the Cliffs of Dover Room, had a booth around the corner from the guild's. In addition to publishing quilting books, they put out the most widely read quilting magazine in the country, a distinction that Cassie Terhune was prepared to challenge, according to Marlene Oxley. Tess hadn't had much chance to talk to them since their arrival. Phyllis, a tall woman in her early fifties who wore too much makeup, hadn't come down with her husband for breakfast that morning. Julian, who was shorter than his wife and who appeared to be in his sixties, had hair too black not to be dyed and a bushy black mustache dusted with gray. He had eaten quickly, saying little to his breakfast-table companions and turning completely mute after Cassie Terhune joined the group. A few minutes later, Julian left the table and took a cup of coffee back upstairs for his wife.

The tension over the breakfast table for those few minutes had been noticable to Tess, but it would have been worse had Rex Brindle's peppery presence been added to the stew. Fortunately, Rex had ventured downstairs after Cassie's departure. By design, Tess surmised.

By craning her neck, Tess could see the Hydes' books and copies of their magazine, a high-quality, glossy publication, displayed in their booth. They seemed to be doing a steady business.

Once, as Phyllis passed the Drunkard's Path booth, a frown of deep reflection on her face, Tess called to her, "Your booth seems to be attracting a lot of customers, Phyllis."

Looking Tess's way, Phyllis responded, "Oh, hi, Tess. I didn't see you there."

"You were lost in thought."

"Just wondering how Cassie Terhune's book sales were going. Between you and me, I sneaked by her booth to check it out. There's a line for her new book." Her expression turned grim. "Of course, Cassie could sell deep freezes to Eskimos." She had returned to her booth then, leaving Tess to ponder on her words.

Letitia Lattimore, another Iris House guest, with whom Tess hadn't had the opportunity to exchange more than idle snippets of conversation, was chatting with several customers when Tess's roving gaze located her booth near the middle of the hall. From what little she'd seen of Letitia, Tess knew she'd like her. Letitia was about sixty and wore her mouse-brown hair up in a bun. A plain woman, she had gray-green eyes and a prominent nose and wore no makeup. But her cheerful manner and a ready smile seemed to brighten any room she entered. And the graceful way she'd handled Cassie Terhune's snideness yesterday had earned her Tess's respect.

During the morning, Tess spotted Shannon Diamond at various booths around the hall, examining merchandise and making a few purchases. Except for occasional trips to the concession stand or rest room, Rex Brindle, Cassie Terhune, and Marlene Oxley remained in their booths all morning, behaving themselves and keeping out of one another's way. Rex and Cassie were scheduled to conduct back-to-back workshops between eleven and one in the room beyond the concession area.

Marlene Oxley had said at breakfast that she would examine the quilts entered in the competition that evening, after the show was closed to the public. Tomorrow, ribbons would be attached to the winning entries.

A welcome lull occurred from noon to one, when fewer

people roamed the hall and the noise level was less than it had been all morning. Tess left the Drunkard's Path booth long enough to go to the pay phone near the concession stand and call Iris House. Nedra Yates, the housekeeper, answered and assured Tess, in a few sparse sentence fragments—Nedra's characteristic mode of communication—that everything was fine at the house and she'd be sure the doors were locked when she left.

"Are you going to make it to the quilt show later?" Tess asked.

"Might."

"You should try, Nedra. You'd enjoy it."

"Prob'ly."

Tess sighed and hung up. Conversing with Nedra was like picking apples from precariously high branches, one by one. Next, she called Luke, who promised he'd be there by one-thirty to relieve her. Another of the quilt guild members had taken Mary Franks's place at the admission ticket table. Tess didn't see Mary anywhere and wondered if she'd gone out for lunch.

When she returned to the booth, Miranda and Kendra were impatient for a break, too. Kendra wore a sulky expression. "Maybe she forgot us," she was saying to Miranda.

"Well, I'm not waiting much longer," Miranda said. "I'm starving." Noticing Tess's return, she came over to the Drunkard's Path booth. "Have you seen Shannon?"

"Not in the last few minutes," Tess said. "I saw her earlier."

"I think it's rude to invite a person to lunch and then forget all about it," Miranda said, glowering around the hall.

"Yeah, *really*!" exclaimed Kendra, who had followed Miranda to Tess's booth.

"I doubt that she's forgotten," Tess said. In fact, Tess

was sure that spending time with Miranda was too important to Shannon for her to forget, though she couldn't have said exactly *why* she was so sure. "Give her a little while. She'll probably be along soon."

"Well, *I* think—"

Tess was never to know what Miranda Franks thought at that point in time, because at that exact moment a horrendously loud crashing noise filled the hall, followed by a woman's scream. Around the hall, heads swiveled toward the sound. Hastily, Tess hid the cash box beneath the counter and left the booth. She had to cover a good distance to see around the tall partition, put up earlier that morning, which screened off the stairs to the loft and the area near it. A pile of two-by-fours lay in the screened-off area. The noise had been the boards falling from the loft to the concrete floor below.

Mary Franks lay on the floor near the stairs. With a gasp, Tess ran toward Mary. As she came nearer, she saw Mary reach for the iron-pipe banister next to the steps leading to the loft and pull herself shakily to her feet. Tess released her held breath in a rush of pure relief. Mary's face was pale, and she struggled to catch her breath, but she didn't seem to be badly hurt.

Running, Tess reached her before anyone else. "Mary, are you all right?"

Mary was still hanging on to the banister. She looked dazed. "I—I think so."

Tess took her arm and led her to the bottom step of the staircase. "Here, sit down. Tell me what happened."

"I don't know. I—" Mary lowered herself carefully to the stairs and repressed a shudder. She hugged herself tightly.

"Take a couple of deep breaths," Tess advised.

Mary did, then said, "I'd been in the rest room and was returning to the admission table, when I had the weirdest

feeling. Like—like the prickling of the hair on your scalp."
She held both hands over her mouth, as though to stop
herself screaming again at the memory. Tess hoped Mary
wasn't going to have hysterics. But, after a moment, Mary
dropped her hands and went on. "A premonition, I guess
you could call it, a sense that something bad was going to
happen. And then, I don't know why, but I looked up at
the loft and saw the boards teetering and I—" She paused
to take a few deep breaths. "I ran and I guess I tripped,
because I fell and then I heard that God-awful noise of the
boards hitting the floor—right where I'd been seconds before—and I screamed." She shuddered.

Tess sat down and put an arm around her shoulders.
"Thank goodness you're all right."

Mary looked at her, two deep vertical lines, like scars
from a sharp knife, etched between her brows. "I don't
understand, Tess. How could those boards have fallen?
When we were up there yesterday, they were stacked several feet from the edge of the loft."

Before Tess could respond, Miranda rushed up, her face
red and agitated. "Mama," she wailed, "are you OK?"

Mary made an obvious effort to compose herself. "I'm
fine, honey. I saw the boards falling and I got scared and
screamed, that's all."

A small crowd was gathering near the stairs. Tess saw
the Hydes and Letitia Lattimore standing together, talking
in hushed voices. Rex Brindle had ventured out of his
booth, as had Cassie Terhune and Marlene Oxley. And
Shannon Diamond stood at the back of the group, craning
to see between the people in front of her.

"Where'd those boards come from?" a high female
voice inquired.

"Up there, I think," a man replied, pointing to the loft.
"Where?"

"They ought to have a guard rail or something," a cross-sounding older woman said. "Somebody could have been killed."

The awful truth of her words struck Tess with full force. Mary *had* very nearly been killed, or badly injured. For a split second, she saw the claw hammer teetering on top of the booth partition as it had last evening when Mary had caught it just in time to keep it from falling. Was Mary one of those people to whom accidents just seemed to happen? Tess glanced at Mary, whose face was regaining its color. She would be all right, and the situation needed to be diffused as quickly as possible. Tess stood, faced the crowd, and said in a calm, strong voice, "Fortunately, nobody was hurt. We'll find a custodian to move those boards out of the way."

Mumbling to one another, the crowd began to disperse. "Mary," Tess asked, "would you like to go home?"

Mary hesitated an instant before she straightened her shoulders and rose to her feet. "I can't. I have to stay at the admission table."

"We can find a substitute for you."

Mary shook her head. "No. I'll have a sandwich and a cup of coffee, and I'll be fine, Tess. Really."

Shannon Diamond hadn't left with the others. Now she came forward to say, "Miranda, maybe you'd rather stay and have lunch with your mother. I was just coming to get you and Kendra when the boards fell."

It occurred to Tess to wonder if Shannon was making a point of stating that she had been elsewhere when the boards toppled off the loft.

Miranda hesitated, peering into her mother's face. "Mama, you want me to stay?"

"Nonsense," Mary said. "You girls go on with Shannon. I know how much you've been looking forward to it."

"Why don't you join us?" Shannon suggested.

Mary shook her head. "Thanks, Shannon, but I can't. I need to be here to oversee things. I'll get something at the concession stand."

Shannon didn't move. "We could stay and eat with you."

Mary gave her a curious look. "That's not necessary, Shannon, and I don't want to disappoint the girls."

Shannon pressed her lips together and made no more suggestions. But she'd apparently planted doubt in Miranda's mind. "Are you sure it's OK if we go with Shannon?" Miranda asked, watching her mother with an expression of distress. Tess's heart went out to the girl. Having lost her father, she must have wondered many times what would happen to her if she lost her mother, too. And it could have happened just now, had Mary been less alert.

"I'm sure." Mary shooed her daughter away with a wave of her hand. "Go on now, and have a good time."

As Shannon and the two girls left, the woman who had been at the admission table when Tess passed it to get to the pay phone, appeared with a custodian in a gray uniform. Her name was Hilda. Tess couldn't remember her last name. "Mr. Snodgrass is going to move those boards out of the way."

Snodgrass, a beefy, middle-aged man with a crewcut so short his gleaming scalp was visible, scowled at the lumber. "I'm gonna get what-for from my boss." He squinted at Mary, who was still sitting on the steps. "You OK, ma'am?"

Mary nodded as she smoothed her red corduroy skirt.

"You ain't gonna sue me or nothin', are you?"

"It wasn't your fault, Mr. Snodgrass," Mary said. "I'm certainly not going to sue you, or anybody else." She darted a glance at Tess before adding, "Accidents happen."

Snodgrass relaxed his uneasy stance. "Can't figure how them boards could've fell. I had 'em stacked a good ways back from the edge, but I'll put 'em even farther back this time.''

"Maybe you should consider adding a guard rail when you have the time,'' Tess suggested.

"I'll speak to the boss about it.'' Snodgrass walked over to the lumber pile and stood staring at it and scratching his head.

"Well, Hilda,'' Mary said with a weak smile, "do you feel like getting back to business?''

"If you do.''

Mary smoothed back her tight, brown curls with both hands, as if wiping away the memory of her close call. "Look, I know you haven't had lunch yet, Hilda. Go ahead and I'll take over the table. You coming, Tess?''

"In a minute,'' Tess said. As soon as the women were out of sight behind the partition, she started up the stairs.

"Hey, where you goin'?'' Snodgrass asked sharply.

"Something I need to do in the loft.'' Tess ran the rest of the way up to the loft, her steps muffled by the stairs' rubber treads. A moment later, she heard Snodgrass's heavy feet on the stairs. He stepped into the loft, carried a board to the back, and dropped it against the wall. The loud, cracking sound made Tess cringe.

"They sure ain't gonna fall from back here,'' he said emphatically as he left to get another board. As he reached the steps, he flipped on the light, a single ceiling bulb.

Standing in the center of the loft, Tess surveyed the area. Boards and varying sizes of panels and screens were stored there for the use of people who rented space in the hall. Two two-by-fours lay side by side perhaps five feet from the open edge of the floor, the only boards left of the pile that had crashed into the hall. Tess had been in the loft yesterday with Mary to get a partition for the Drunkard's Path booth. At that time, Mary had contemplated taking a couple of boards, too, but had decided to wait and see if they could get along without them.

Tess closed her eyes and tried to envision the neatly stacked pile of boards as they had been yesterday when Mary called them to her attention. Her recollection was the same as Mary's. Five or six feet of bare floor space separated the pile from the edge of the loft. The two boards remaining in the loft were evidence that her recollection was accurate.

Snodgrass came in with another board and dropped it with a clatter beside the one he'd already placed against the wall. This time, Tess was ready for the noise and braced herself.

"What're you doing?" he asked suspiciously.

Tess shook her head. "Just thinking." If the boards had been piled haphazardly, it was conceivable that one of them could have moved, shifting the whole stack closer to the edge and causing them to fall. But Tess had a clear memory of three neat stacks of boards, each board placed squarely atop the one below it. There was no way they could have fallen on their own.

Had somebody helped them?

She turned to the custodian, who was still watching her guardedly. Perhaps he thought she was looking for evidence to be used in a lawsuit. "Mr. Snodgrass, is there more than one way to get to the loft?"

He studied her for another moment before saying grudgingly, "A door back in the corner there"—he pointed—"and an outside staircase leading to the ground. But that door's usually kept locked." He turned and clambered loudly down the stairs.

Snodgrass, Tess decided, was the noisiest man she'd ever met. She walked to the area he had pointed out. As Tess drew close, she could make out the snug-fitting door. The loft was so poorly lighted that she hadn't noticed it before. She turned the knob. It opened easily. Stepping out on a small landing, she gazed down the outside stairs and scanned the ground all around. Except for a few pieces of innocuous litter—a crumpled cigarette package, a Hershey wrapper, a scrap of newspaper—she saw nothing.

Stepping back inside, she closed the door and leaned back against it, thinking. Since the boards couldn't have moved themselves, someone had been in the loft and had accidentally, or purposely, dislodged the stack of boards and sent them over the edge.

After a few moments of pondering, she returned to where the two remaining boards of the original stack lay. She bent over to examine the floor, hoping to find a trace of dusty footprints, but Snodgrass was a good housekeeper. The loft floor was clean.

Yet Tess thought somebody had definitely been here only a few minutes earlier. Perhaps they'd entered by the outside stairs. It was almost certain they'd left that way. It was conceivable, Tess supposed, that they could have run down the inside stairs after pushing the boards and returned to the hall before Tess got far enough to see all the area behind the partition. But Mary would have seen them, and if she had she certainly would have mentioned it.

Tess closed her eyes, imagining a figure standing in the loft just minutes earlier, standing there and waiting for the right moment to push the boards off the loft. But it was a shadowy figure without a face.

More troubled than before, Tess went back downstairs, now fully convinced the boards could not have fallen without help.

Had somebody tried to kill Mary Franks?

Chapter 6

It was close to two when Luke finally arrived at the exhibition hall, full of apologies. "I'm sorry I didn't get here when I said I would, sweetheart. The computer repairman was late, and I had to wait and let him into the office."

They were seated on a bench at one of the long redwood picnic tables near the concession stand with hamburgers, coffee, and a couple of Gertie's Scrumptious Chocolate Chip Cookies. Gertie had made sure Luke got the biggest cookie, Tess noticed.

Hilda was again manning the admissions table; Mary Franks was feeling better and had taken over the Drunkard's Path booth for half an hour so Tess and Luke could have lunch together. "Are your computers down?" Tess asked, still distracted by the conclusion she'd reached in the loft, that a would-be killer was on the loose.

"One of them. I always try to keep two in running order. I can't afford to be cut off when the market is trading."

With an effort, Tess pulled her mind away from sinister, shadow figures without faces, to attend to what Luke was saying. "Sort of like wearing a belt *and* suspenders. Doesn't sound like you, Luke. What happened to going with the flow?"

"Doesn't apply when it comes to keeping in touch with Wall Street," Luke said with all seriousness and bit into his hamburger. Keeping his eyes on Tess's face, he took a drink of coffee, then set his mug down. "OK, what's wrong?"

"Wrong?"

"You've been preoccupied ever since I got here, Tess."

"All right. It's true," she admitted.

"You miffed at me for being late?"

"No, it isn't that."

"Is there a problem at Iris House?"

She shook her head. "Nedra says things are fine there. At least I think that was the gist of the two or three words I pulled out of her."

Luke smiled. "Be thankful Nedra's not a chatterer. That could be even more trying in an employee. Now, you were saying?"

"Something happened in the exhibition hall earlier." She told him about Mary Franks's close call and described her own examination of the loft under Snodgrass's suspicious scrutiny.

"Maybe it's because I know how your mind works, Tess, but I get a feeling you don't think it was an accident."

"Mary called it an accident," Tess confessed, "but I'm not sure she believes it. And I don't see how it could be."

Luke lifted his shoulders. "It sounds like the most logical explanation to me. Maybe the two-by-fours were closer to the edge of the loft than you remember from yesterday. One of those heavy doors banging shut on the ground floor might have caused enough of a vibration to dislodge them." He ate a bite of his burger and wiped his mouth with a paper napkin. "You're right, though. There should be a guard rail or, better yet, a solid wall along the edge of the loft. I'll see what I can do about that." The Chamber of Commerce was in charge of the Civic Center facilities. In effect, the salaried manager of the center worked for them. As chairman of the board, Luke could get the other members' approval in a few minutes over the telephone. After they heard what had happened today, they'd want to take precautions as soon as the quilt show closed. "I'll take care of it when I get back to the office," he added.

Tess was glad something would be done right away, but it didn't stop her worrying about Mary Franks. "I didn't say this to Mary, Luke, but I think somebody's got it in for Mary. Somebody tried to kill her."

He heaved a sigh, as if to say he was afraid of that. "Now, Tess, I know you're upset about what happened, but don't get carried away. Who would want to kill Mary Franks?"

That was, indeed, the question. Tess could not imagine that Mary had ever done anything in her life to make someone hate her enough to want to kill her. "I don't know," she admitted.

"If it was intentional," Luke said in a clearly doubtful tone, "then whoever did it had to go up to the loft and push the boards off. Did you see anybody up there, or coming down the stairs after it happened?"

"No. But with that partition up, you can't see the stairs unless you're on that side of the partition, too. Besides, there's another way out of the loft."

Luke's expression turned thoughtful. "The back staircase," he said finally. "I'd forgotten about it."

"I checked, and it's not locked."

"Maybe the fire marshal requires that it be open when the hall is occupied," Luke said. "I'll check that out."

Tess was still thinking about the outside stairs. Whoever

had pushed those boards off could easily have run down that staircase and returned to the hall by any one of several doors along each side and joined the crowd around Mary without anyone noticing.

"I still can't believe somebody wants to kill Mary," Luke mused.

"It was *no* accident, Luke," Tess insisted.

Luke finished off his hamburger pensively. Then, "OK, assume those boards were pushed off the loft. Isn't it possible the culprit mistook Mary for somebody else?"

Tess sighed. "Maybe, but added to what happened last evening . . ." Her voice trailed off.

His eyes were alert. "When you and Mary were working in the guild's booth?"

"Yes. Shannon Diamond was there, too. And that's another troubling thing." She frowned abstractedly. "Which I'll explain later." Luke frowned, too, as he tried to follow the quick turns of her conversation.

"About last night," Tess went on, "Mary had brought a big claw hammer from home. Mary remembered leaving it on the booth counter, and I recall seeing it there at some point, though I can't remember the time. Anyway, shortly before I left to get ready for dinner, Mary started looking for the hammer. Shannon and I both helped her search. When I bent down and put a hand on one of the booth partitions, Mary yelled for me not to move." Luke's brows rose, but he remained silent. "She'd located the hammer—on top of the partition," Tess continued. "It was just teetering there. She reached up and grabbed it, barely kept it from falling on my head. We couldn't figure out how it got there in the first place or how long it had been there."

"Somebody was careless," Luke suggested.

"I thought that's all there was to it, too, before what happened today. But now I wonder if the hammer wasn't placed there in hopes it would fall on Mary. Everyone involved in the quilt show knew she'd be in the booth all day, and they were all in the hall at some time during the day and could have put the hammer on the partition when Mary stepped away from the booth.''

"But you were there, too."

"Not all day, Luke. And, like Mary, I came and went. Besides, who would want a hammer to fall on me?"

"Can't think of a soul," Luke admitted with a wry grin. He sobered quickly. "But I repeat, I can't think of anybody who'd want to hurt Mary Franks, either."

Yet somebody obviously did. Voicing her thoughts had only solidified Tess's conviction. She munched on her cookie in glum silence and thought about Shannon Diamond's clear but incomprehensible interest in Mary and Miranda Franks. She gazed into the distance, over Luke's shoulder. Was Shannon carrying a grudge against the Franks, especially Mary? It seemed hardly within the realm of possibility, since neither Mary nor Miranda had met Shannon before yesterday. Or if they had crossed paths with her sometime in the past, they didn't remember it, which meant that it hadn't been a significant encounter—to Mary and Miranda, at any rate. But perhaps it had been significant to Shannon.

Tess felt a chill. Had Shannon Diamond pushed those boards off the loft?

"Where are you, dearest?" Luke queried.

Tess brought her gaze back to Luke's intent blue eyes. "Just thinking."

"Well, think about this. It's pretty farfetched to imagine that someone would have put the hammer on top of the partition in hopes of hurting Mary. I mean, Mary would have had to be in the right place and the hammer would have to land exactly so to do much damage. That's a pretty inefficient way of trying to hurt someone."

"I know, but maybe it was only meant to warn Mary."

"Warn her of what? That she shouldn't mislay her hammer?"

"You aren't taking this seriously, Luke."

"Yes, I am," he protested. "Go on with what you mentioned before. You said you'd explain something about Shannon Diamond."

"Oh, that." Tess told him of Shannon's curiosity about the Franks, her offering to stay and help Mary with the booth last night, her questioning Gertie that morning, her invitation to lunch for Miranda and Miranda's friend, and, after Mary's close escape, her eagerness to have Mary join them for lunch.

While she talked, Luke ate his cookie, his eyes never leaving her face. When she paused, he said, "It's curious, but not sinister. What do you make of it?"

Tess threw out her hands. "Nothing sensible, that's the problem. I don't have a clue what's going on in Shannon's mind. I just keep getting the eerie feeling that she's after something or up to something . . ." She heaved a sigh. "Actually, I'm totally baffled. But I intend to talk to Mary about Shannon."

He considered this in silence. Then, he said tentatively, "Maybe you should stay out of it."

"Oh, I will," she said airily, waving a hand, "after I've talked to Mary. I want to know if *she* thinks Shannon's interest in her and Miranda is as odd as Gertie and I do."

"OK," Luke said, if a bit reluctantly. "I can see I might as well save my breath." He gathered up their litter. "I'd better go and relieve Mary at the booth. Why don't you sit here and rest for a while."

She nodded gratefully. Luke looked around for a trash bin. "It's over there," Tess told him, pointing.

"Ah, now I see it." He gazed at her fondly. "Come in and keep me company in a while. I'll find you a chair."

"I'll be there in a few minutes."

Luke started toward the trash bin.

Suddenly the lights went out, plunging the windowless hall into darkness as black as tar.

There was a woman's high-pitched squeal. It was followed by a moment of silence, then other voices rose in consternation and bewilderment.

"What's going on?"

"Somebody turn on the lights!"

"Anybody know where the circuit breakers are?" a man's voice yelled.

"Yo," replied another man. "Give me a minute. I'll try to feel my way over there."

Tess had noticed the breaker box earlier. It was near the main entrance door, not far from the Drunkard's Path booth.

There was the sound of feet shuffling and a gasp of pain as somebody near Tess stumbled into a table in the dark and mumbled an oath. Then there was a solid thump and the sound of something crashing to the floor.

"Everybody just be calm," shouted a male voice. "Stay right where you are until we can get some light in here."

Someone brushed against Tess. She pulled back. "Sorry."

"It's just me, love," said Luke near her ear. She heard him depositing their litter on the table. He hadn't made it to the trash bin.

Tess felt a chill at the back of her neck. Exactly the feeling Mary Franks had described before she looked up and saw a pile of boards rushing toward her.

A premonition, Mary had called it, like a prickling of the scalp.

A foreboding, Tess thought.

She grabbed his hand. "Come on, Luke," she said urgently.

He pulled back on her hand, keeping her there. "That fellow had it right, Tess. The best thing we can do is stay where we are until they get the lights back on."

"We have to get to the Drunkard's Path booth *now*! Mary's in danger. If we wait, it may be too late." This time when she tugged at him, he followed her, moved by the panic in her voice. With Tess feeling the way with her free hand, they progressed with agonizing slowness toward the booth.

Chapter 7

"What was that noise?" Miranda Franks shrilled. "It sounded like something fell, over here somewhere. Somebody—"

"Everyone stay where you are!"

"I'm scared!" That quavery voice sounded like Kendra's.

Hurrying, Tess ran into something hard and yelped in pain.

"You OK?" Luke asked.

"Yes. I found the door." It was the facing that she'd smacked into. "We've only a little farther to go." What was that thump and the crashing sound she'd heard? Miranda had said it was near her, near the home ec booth. Tess's anxiety revved up. *Dear heaven*, she thought, *let me be wrong!* She couldn't stand not knowing any longer. "Mary," she yelled. "Mary Franks!"

In the hush that followed Tess's shout, a voice replied from a good distance away. "I'm back here. Who's calling me?"

Thank God, Mary's all right. The quivering tension in Tess ebbed a little. Mary must have had to leave the booth before the lights went out. That may have saved her life. "It's me. Tess."

"Will you people stay calm and shut up!" It sounded like the man who'd volunteered to find the breaker box.

Tess touched a counter, ran her hand along it until she felt the metal cash box. At least she knew where she was now. She'd found the Drunkard's Path booth. Had Mary left the cash box unattended? No, it wasn't like Mary to be so careless; she'd probably asked Miranda to keep an eye on it.

"Miranda?" Tess called.

"We're here. Is that you, Tess?" Miranda's voice quavered somewhere to Tess's right.

"Yes," Tess said. "Where did that noise come from?"

"It sounded like it was over there. I think something in that booth fell over."

"Scared us to death!" Kendra wailed. "I was like yikes, the roof's caving in!"

"Somebody must've run into a partition," Tess replied. She released Luke's hand, felt her way around the counter, and took a tentative step into the Drunkard's Path booth. "Is anybody here?" she asked softly. There was no answer.

So why couldn't she shake the feeling of a presence?

Tess took more cautious steps deeper into the booth. Her shin hit something solid. Feeling with her hand, she identified it as a partition like the ones she and Mary had used for the back and sides of the booth. She felt suddenly cold. The partition was sturdy with a wide base. It couldn't have fallen all by itself. It had to have help.

Just like the boards, she thought.

Tess straightened up. "Miranda," she called, "did you or Kendra bump against a partition?"

"Not me," Miranda replied.

"Me, either. I hate this," Kendra whimpered. "When are they going to get the lights back on?"

"Hey, I found the box!" a triumphant male voice announced. "The main breaker's off. Must've been overloaded. Just a minute . . ."

Abruptly, light flooded the hall. There was a communal sigh of relief and a few laughs as people began to talk and move about. Luke was standing just outside the booth.

Blinking against the sudden brightness, Tess turned and saw Mary Franks hurrying toward them from the center of the hall. Sandra Patterson was standing in The Quilter's Nook booth, both hands braced against the counter.

Miranda and Kendra came out of the home ec booth and stopped beside Luke, as if for the comfort of another human being—a strong, male human being. Tess still stood next to the fallen partition. It was the one that had formed the booth's back wall. A hunter-green corner of the Drunkard's Path quilt that was being raffled stuck out from beneath the partition. The far side of the partition rested on the floor, but the edge that Tess had bumped into was a good two feet off the floor. There was something else under it, something much thicker than the quilt. Not the rocking chair. It stood, undisturbed, in the corner. It wasn't the quilt rack, either. The rack had fallen on its side, probably toppled by the falling partition. Then, what—?

Before Tess's thought could crystallize, Luke came around the counter and, grasping the partition with both hands, lifted it upright.

Miranda screamed, a high-pitched sound that went on and on. Against the background of Miranda's screaming, Kendra began to sob.

Having righted the partition, Luke released it and stepped back. Then he looked down and halted, frozen to the spot by what he saw. "Good God."

Tess reached out and clung to his arm. There was more blood than she had ever seen before. A big section of the Drunkard's Path quilt was soaked with it. Cassie Terhune lay on her back, her lifeless eyes staring, unseeing, at the ceiling. She must have grabbed the quilt when she fell, bringing down both the quilt and the partition. Blood covered her throat; it had been slit very nearly from ear to ear. Near her lay a quilter's rotary cutter, its large-sized, circular blade smeared with crimson.

Miranda finally stopped screaming and began to cry softly in the ensuing, eerie silence. Mere seconds had passed since Tess saw the body and Miranda started screaming, but it seemed like an eternity. Tess had an irrational impulse to run to the breaker box and turn the lights off again, as if she could make time go backward and resurrect Cassie.

Sandra Patterson left The Quilter's Nook booth and came over to Tess. "What on earth—?" Then she saw the body. "Oh, no! Who— what—" Words failed her, until she noticed the murder weapon. Her hand flew to her mouth and she darted a horrified look at Tess. "That can't be . . . I mean, could that rotary cutter have come from the basket in my booth?"

Tess thought it was virtually a certainty, but she said, "I don't know, Sandra. Did you hear anyone at your booth after the lights went out?"

Sandra looked away from the body, her face pinched. "I'm not sure. People were moving about all over the hall, in spite of that man telling them to stay put." She took a deep breath and shook her head forlornly. "That poor woman. She was a friend of Mary's, wasn't she?"

Tess nodded.

"I noticed she was taking Mary's place in the booth right before the lights went out." Sandra darted another glance at the body and backed away. "I—I have to get a drink of water."

As Sandra left, Mary Franks pushed into the Drunkard's Path booth beside Tess, who heard her sudden gasp of shock before she turned to see Mary herself. Mary had turned ashen. She teetered precariously. Tess grabbed hold of Mary's waist to keep her from falling.

"Cassie!" Mary's cry was anguished. "Oh, Cassie, no . . ." She fell to her knees beside the body. "Oh, Cassie, why? Why?" She looked up at Tess. "Do something! We have to help her."

"Nobody can help her now," Tess murmured. "Luke, Mary needs to sit down."

"I was only gone a few minutes. Oh, this is my fault. I should never have left her alone in the booth!"

If she hadn't, Tess thought grimly, she'd probably be the one lying there with her throat cut. Tess helped her to stand, patted her shoulder in a feeble effort to soothe her. "How could you have known, Mary?"

Luke put an arm around Mary and, ignoring her continued protests, led her away.

Other people had reached the booth now, among them Marlene Oxley and Rex Brindle. Marlene was crying soundlessly and Rex was awkwardly trying to comfort her.

Tess started to shake. She had seen dead bodies before, even the bodies of murder victims. But she had never seen anything like this.

So much blood.

She swallowed the gorge that rose in her throat and abruptly turned away from the gruesome sight. She didn't understand what was happening. Who on earth was doing these evil things?

Miranda and Kendra watched her apprehensively, as if they expected her to do something to make things right. But nothing would ever be right for Cassie Terhune again.

"Miranda," Tess said, "you and Kendra should go find your mother. See if she needs anything." She knew that Mary was in Luke's capable hands, but she wanted to get the girls away from this horror. They seemed grateful to be sent away.

The custodian Snodgrass's bulky form shouldered into

the booth. He stared down at the body and his face turned gray. "What in hell is going on around here?" He continued to stare at the body as though he couldn't comprehend what he was seeing. "A nasty business," he pronounced finally, shaking his head. "This show is jinxed." Then he seemed to shake himself and yelled at the crowd, "Somebody call the police."

"My husband's already gone to do it." That was Phyllis Hyde.

Snodgrass bent down beside the body.

"We shouldn't touch anything," Tess said sharply.

He looked up at her and swallowed hard. "I ain't gonna touch nothin'." He struggled to his feet. "And neither is anybody else, till the police get here. Nobody better leave, either." He planted himself four-square in the booth's opening, his feet spread, his arms crossed like boulders across his chest.

The crowd gazed at him. Nobody moved.

Leaving Snodgrass to guard the booth, Tess went in search of Luke. She found him near the bank of glass doors leading from the concession area outside. "I'm waiting for the police," he said. "Chief Butts was in a car wreck last Sunday and has a broken leg. I don't know if he's back at work yet or who might be in charge in his absence."

Tess shivered and he put his arm around her. "Where's Mary?" Tess asked.

"Lying down on a bench in the other room. She's taking this awfully hard, but she'll be all right. It was the shock . . ." He pressed Tess closer against his side.

"She's had more than her share of those today."

He nodded. "Miranda's with her now."

Tess looked up at him. "I don't pretend to understand what's happening, Luke. But it's possible whoever did this killed the wrong person."

"We can't be sure, love."

"The killer must have thought Cassie was Mary," Tess persisted.

"Maybe so, Tess. Mary was supposed to be in the booth until I came to relieve her. She told me that Cassie had come by to see if she could take a coffee break. But Mary wasn't feeling well. A tension headache. She gets them periodically, she said."

"She's certainly been under stress today. I knew she should have gone home after the boards fell," Tess murmured. "If only she had . . ."

"Cassie thought she should leave, too, but Mary refused. So Cassie insisted that she find some aspirin and lie down on the couch in the ladies' room," Luke continued. "Cassie volunteered to stay in the booth until I came to relieve her." He was thoughtful for a moment. "None of the fuses in the circuit box was blown."

"And the lights haven't gone off again," Tess added, "which they would have if they were overloaded. Somebody turned off the breaker." As if they needed any other proof than Cassie's body.

"It would seem so," Luke murmured.

Tess felt jittery, as though she should be doing something useful. "Snodgrass is guarding the body," she said. "I think I'll go back and keep him company."

She returned to the hall, stopping just inside to gaze at the breaker box to the right of the door. Standing with her back to it, she tried to determine which booths had a view of the box—and anybody who approached it. Though the Drunkard's Path booth, to the right of the main entrance, and the two booths flanking it were close to the breaker box, to the left of the entrance, a person standing in any one of them would have his view obstructed by the tall partition forming the side of the booth to the left of the door and nearest to the breaker box. The same partition also screened the box from the view of anybody in that booth.

In fact, only somebody standing or walking in the main aisle just inside the entrance could have seen the person who turned the breaker off and plunged the hall into darkness. Tess was pretty sure they would find no such witness. The killer would have waited, out of sight behind the booths to the left of the door, until the coast was clear. From there, he would not have seen Mary leave the Drunkard's Path booth and Cassie Terhune take her place.

From the circuit box to the Drunkard's Path booth was but a few steps. The killer could have taken the rotary cutter earlier or he could have noticed the basket earlier and grabbed a cutter in the darkness as he passed Sandra Patterson's booth.

But *if* the killer thought Mary was in the booth, *who* on earth could it be? Who would want to slit Mary's throat, and why? And why now? Mary had lived in Victoria Springs for two years. If the killer lived there, too, he could easily have found a far less risky time and place to do away with her when there weren't so many people around. It was difficult to escape the conclusion that the killer didn't live in Victoria Springs, but had come there to kill Mary. The quilt show would serve as the perfect cover for the killer's presence in town.

Shannon Diamond came to mind because of her behavior toward Mary. But, no, it had to be somebody who'd known Mary before she moved to Victoria Springs. That was the only thing that made any sense to Tess. But did that exclude Shannon? She could have known Mary in the past and, for some reason, be pretending *not* to know her. Whether or not Shannon had known Mary before, the killer must have, and that narrowed the pool of suspects considerably. Mary had been friends with Cassie Terhune and Marlene Oxley for years. And she'd known Rex Brindle; last night, she'd told Mary what a braggart he'd been when he began attending quilting events. Since Mary had been active in quilting circles most of her adult life, she almost certainly had come in contact with Letitia Lattimore and the Hydes in the past, too.

As for the puzzling Shannon Diamond, she might not be a killer but she clearly had her own agenda when it came to Mary Franks. Tess was determined to find out what it was.

Most of those who'd originally crowded around the Drunkard's Path booth remained rooted to the spot, held by the all-too-human fascination with tragedy. Tess scanned faces.

Letitia Lattimore stood toward the front of the group but to one side, as if she wanted to separate herself from the gawkers, but couldn't bring herself to leave, either. Her intelligent gray-green eyes were narrowed in thought, as though she was carefully working through a knotty problem, like unraveling a snarl in quilting thread. Tess would have loved to know what Letitia was thinking. Then Letitia's eyes locked with Tess's, and the creases alongside her mouth deepened, making her look older as well as troubled and a little frightened. Letitia's gaze shifted and she looked down at the toes of her comfortable, lace-up black oxfords.

Julian Hyde's dyed black hair stood up in back, as if he'd slept on it wrong. He was in the middle of the gathering, his posture straight, his chin raised, his neck stretched, so that he could see over the head of the woman in front of him. One arm was crossed over his midriff, the other elbow propped on it, the hand positioned to smooth his mustache at frequent intervals, an unconscious gesture that Tess had seen him make before.

Phyllis Hyde, half a head taller than her husband, had a clear view of Snodgrass, who stood like a statue in the booth opening, shielding the body from view, his broad cheeks flushed a ruddy-red, from extreme anxiety or anger—Tess couldn't tell which. Perhaps he was irate because somebody had had the gall to commit murder in a building for which he was responsible. Phyllis's brown eyes were alert, shrewd, her expression showing little shock and no regret. She was simply waiting for what would transpire.

Rex Brindle had moved away from Marlene Oxley, away from the bulk of the spectators, and now slouched against a wall, his hands in his trouser pockets, one leg crossed over the other, knee bent, the toe of his loafer resting on the floor. He looked as unconcerned as if he were waiting for a bus. Occasionally he glanced at Snodgrass impassively.

Marlene Oxley's arms were wrapped around her body, as if to protect herself from a sudden drop in temperature. Her eyes were red, her face tinged a sickly green. Her gaze shifted nervously from one spot to another, never settling in one place for long and never alighting anywhere near Snodgrass or the bloody body lying behind him.

Belatedly, Tess found herself looking for evidence of blood on people's clothing, but she saw none. The killer had stood behind Cassie Terhune, she surmised, perhaps without Cassie even knowing he was there until it was too late. He could have reached over her shoulder with the rotary cutter and made a swift, hard pass across her throat. If he was quick enough, he could have jumped back before any blood got on his clothing. When Cassie had started to fall, the killer had dropped the murder weapon and left the booth as the partition crashed down behind him. He would have moved as far away as possible before the lights were turned back on, perhaps hugging a wall behind a row of booths, coming out to join the people rushing toward the Drunkard's Path booth.

A siren sounded in the distance and the spectators stiffened, stood straighter. Tess's glance slid to the body, and her stomach lurched. She swallowed hard and looked away.

Hurried footsteps approached. They were accompanied by the rapid thump of crutches. A murmur ran through the crowd.

Chapter 8

The police had arrived. Luke led them into the exhibition hall. Chief of Police Desmond Butts, his right leg in a cast below the knee, stumped along behind him. Butts was followed by a young officer, Andy Neill. Another, older man in a brown suit accompanied them. Two ambulance attendants with a litter brought up the rear. Snodgrass nodded and stepped aside to allow the newcomers to enter the booth.

Butts, bushy-headed and spectacled, with a ruddy, blunt-featured face, scowled at the spectators as he passed Snodgrass. Andy Neill followed closely, his head bowed, in respect for the dead, Tess supposed. Tess had come to know Neill the previous summer, when one of her guests was murdered at a book signing in her cousin Cinny's bookshop. Neill was in his twenties, tall and gangly, with tawny hair and protruding jug ears.

As much as Tess disliked Chief of Police Butts, who usually managed to irritate her within moments of any meeting, she wasn't entirely sorry he was back on duty. She suspected a murder investigation would be too much for Andy Neill and the other young, inexperienced officers on the Victoria Springs force to handle alone.

As the man in the suit bent down beside the body, Butts turned and sent his piercing gaze over the crowd. His eyes halted for a moment on Tess, and his scowl deepened. Last summer, he'd observed to her that she always seemed to be on hand when a murder was committed in Victoria Springs, as though she had some kind of murder radar. It had sounded almost like an accusation, as if he suspected her of being an accessory or something. Of course, his attitude had infuriated her. Which had probably been Butts's intent, as Tess had realized later.

Tess couldn't quite figure Butts out. Luke said, because of growing up "on the wrong side of the tracks," Butts resented the affluent, influential families in town, and since Tess was a Darcy, she was in that category. Tess's great-grandfather had been one of the first to build a big Victorian house on the hill overlooking town, and her grandfather had been mayor of Victoria Springs. Apparently it didn't matter to Butts that she had put everything she had saved and inherited into her bed and breakfast and would be penniless if it failed.

Stiffening her spine, she returned Butts's stare until, finally, his wide mouth formed a sneer and he looked away.

"Who's the man in the suit?" Tess asked Luke. The man in question was still bent over the body, his back to the spectators.

"Dr. Bertrand, the medical examiner."

Chief Butts leaned over and said something to the medical examiner, who nodded and replied without looking up. Then Butts spoke sharply to Andy Neill, who hastily produced a small pad and pen and began making a sketch of the scene. The ambulance attendants waited just outside the booth, the litter they'd carried in lying on the floor at their feet.

Butts turned and motioned imperiously to Tess and Luke. They moved to his side. "Fredrik here says she was staying at your bed and breakfast,'' he said without preamble in a gravelly whisper, jerking a thumb toward the body.

Tess nodded. "That's true."

A muscle in Butts's jaw spasmed. "Well, ain't that dandy? That just about tears it."

"I don't understand. What tears it?"

"The victim's staying at Iris House. It's too damned co-incidental."

"I have no idea what you mean," Tess said with a sniff, though of course she knew perfectly well. Butts was not exactly subtle.

Butts snorted. "Then let me spell it out for you. People around you keep dropping like flies. They don't just die, they get murdered." Before Tess could answer, he asked, "Where's this one from?"

"Kansas City."

"Should've stayed at home." Butts rubbed a beefy hand across his face. "Any other people here from Kansas City that you know of?"

"Marlene Oxley," Tess said. After a pause, during which Butts watched her like a hawk, she said reluctantly, "As it happens, she's staying at Iris House, too."

"Of course she is. What else is new?" When Tess did not respond to his sarcasm, he barked, "Who else is staying at your bed and breakfast?"

"Several people," Tess said. "I have a full house."

"All of 'em involved in this quilt fandangle?"

"Yes."

"They all know the victim?"

"Yes, but, Chief, I'm not sure the killer meant to kill Cassie Terhune."

"Oh, gee, why didn't I think of that? This is some kind of freak accident!"

"I didn't say that. I—"

Butts interrupted rudely. "Hell's bells!" he bellowed.

"There is no way this woman got her throat slit by accident!"

Tess tried not to grind her teeth. "Of course not. What I mean is that I think the killer may have meant to kill Mary Franks." Tess explained as succinctly as possible what had led her to that conclusion.

Butts pushed his glasses up his nose and scratched his chin. He shook his head. "Well, now, maybe I just better turn this murder investigation over to you, you seem to know so much about it."

"I *have* been here the last two days. I've seen what went on."

"Like I said," he growled, "damned coincidental." He leaned on his crutches and cleared his throat portentously. For an instant, Tess feared he meant to spit on the floor. Butts had a nasty habit of spitting, but she'd never seen him do it indoors—yet. Fortunately, Butts didn't indulge himself this time. Apparently, spitting in the exhibition hall was outside even Desmond Butts's rudimentary rules of etiquette.

"I'll bet you knew where the circuit box was, too," he said accusingly.

Luke stepped closer. "Chief, I don't like your insinuations. Tess was with me when this happened."

"Oh, yeah?" Butts said icily. "Where exactly *were* the two of you when this lady got her throat cut from ear to ear?"

All at once, Tess's hamburger was threatening to come up. She swallowed a bitter taste. "Eating lunch," she said finally. "At one of the tables near the concession stand. We were there when the lights went out."

Butts's eyes narrowed. "Tell me you stayed there till they came back on."

Tess sighed and admitted, "Not exactly."

The back of Butts's neck reddened. "Exactly where did you go while the hall was dark?"

"We made our way back toward this booth," Luke inserted sharply. "Tess has been selling raffle tickets here all day."

"As I told you, Mary Franks took my place when I went to lunch," Tess said. "When the lights went out, I had a premonition that they'd been turned off by whoever has been after Mary."

Butts rolled his eyes toward the ceiling. "Premonition. Heaven help us. I don't give a damn about your premonitions! Or your female intuition, either! Bunch of hogwash."

"Except this premonition turned out to be valid, didn't it?" Tess inquired sweetly, rushing on before Butts could get in another insult. "Evidently, the murderer didn't know Mary had left the booth for a few minutes. In the dark, he could easily have killed the wrong person."

"Well, it ain't all that evident to me," Butts grumbled. "Premonitions!" he snorted. "But, just for the novelty of it—" He smiled at Tess with his lips only. "Maybe I'll come at this from both angles. Undertake two investigations, since I got nothing better to do, what with the town full of tourists, half of 'em drunk, the other half so hellbent to get where they're going that they ignore the speed limit." He glared at Tess. "On the teeny weeny off-chance you're right and ain't just carried away by some murder movie you saw on TV . . ." He pulled a small spiral tablet and ballpoint pen from his uniform pocket.

"He's the most insulting man I've ever met," Tess hissed behind her hand to Luke, who nodded an emphatic agreement.

Butts clomped around Tess and Luke and yelled at the crowd, "Anybody hear the victim say anything when she was attacked?" Heads shook. Nobody spoke.

"Nobody heard her scream?"

Again, nobody spoke. "Hmm," Butts muttered. "Maybe that means she knew her killer and trusted him." He raised his voice again. "Now, I want the names of everybody who knew Cassie Terhune before this quilt whatchamacallit started." He pointed a finger in Tess and Luke's direction. "You two stay put, too." He turned and stared at the Drunkard's Path booth. "Plus, I want to talk to the people who were in the two booths on either side of this one. Everybody hear me?"

Of course they had. People in Arkansas, Oklahoma, and Kansas had heard him.

Tess hadn't noticed that Mary Franks had returned to the hall with Miranda and Kendra until she and the two girls stepped forward. Mary was still as pale as a ghost. Then, one by one, Sandra Patterson, Marlene Oxley, Rex Brindle, Letitia Lattimore, and Julian and Phyllis Hyde joined them.

Butts ordered everybody else to vacate the hall, telling them they could leave the center or wait in the concession area to be readmitted to the hall. In the meantime, one of the ambulance attendants had taken a body bag from the litter and Officer Neill had made several sketches and snapped pictures of the scene with a small camera that he'd pulled from a trouser pocket.

When the medical examiner finished his examination, the attendants wrapped the bloody quilt around the body and maneuvered it into the bag, lifted it to the litter, and carried it out. Tess noticed that the murder weapon had been placed in a clear plastic bag. The handle was covered with a powdery substance—evidently Neill had already dusted it for fingerprints. It lay on the booth counter with several other evidence bags collected by Andy Neill.

As the medical examiner prepared to leave, Tess edged closer and eavesdropped unabashedly. "What can you tell me, Doc?" Butts asked.

"Two things," Bertrand said. "The killer was right-handed and taller than the victim. Can't say more than that until I do the autopsy.''

Bertrand left and Butts stumped over to Tess. "How tall was the victim?''

"She was short," Tess said, "maybe five-one or -two.''

"She was five feet two inches tall," Marlene Oxley said. "I've known"—she paused to swallow hard—"er, I knew her for twenty years. She hated being short. She always wanted to be tall and willowy and—'' Her voice broke, and she dabbed at her eyes with the handkerchief balled in her hand. Her nose was beet-red, her lashes moistened by tears and stuck together. "I'm sorry. This is just so horrible. I can't believe anyone would do that to Cassie.''

"Five-two," Butts grumbled. "That's a great big help.''

Tess knew what he was thinking. Everybody in the group of people who'd known Cassie was taller than that, which meant, on that basis alone, any one of them could have killed her. She hadn't paid enough attention to know if any of them was left-handed.

Butts pushed up his glasses with thumb and forefinger and pinched the bridge of his nose. As if reading Tess's thoughts, he demanded, "Anybody here left-handed?'' Nobody responded. "Terrific," Butts mumbled. Then he looked up and barked, "Neill, get me a chair.''

"Yes, sir!'' The young officer spotted a folding chair in the home ec booth and positioned it behind the chief. Neill reached out to help him, but Butts shook off his hand. "I ain't an invalid, dammit!'' He shifted both crutches to one hand and, balancing on one foot, lowered his broad rear end slowly into the chair.

He laid the crutches on the floor and flipped open his tablet. "OK, I want names, addresses, and a phone number where you can be reached in the next few days. And I want to know where each of you was when the lights went out and where you were when they came back on again.''

One by one, they answered the chief's questions.

Rex Brindle and Letitia Lattimore had been in their booths the whole time.

The Hydes had gone to town for lunch and were returning to their booth when the lights went out. The darkness caught them several booths short of their own, and they halted and waited there until light was restored.

A few minutes before the lights went out, Marlene Oxley had passed the Drunkard's Path booth, on her way to the concession stand. Surprised to see Cassie in attendance, she had stopped and asked if she wanted something to drink. Cassie had said to bring her something cold. Then Marlene had continued toward the concession stand, passing through the door where the admission tickets were being sold moments before the lights went out. She edged to one side of the door, the side opposite the ticket table, and waited there, her back to the wall, until the lights came back on.

Mary Franks, upon the insistance of Cassie Terhune, who offered to relieve her in the booth, had gone to the rest room to take an aspirin and lie down on the couch there. After a few minutes, she was feeling better and had started back to the booth. She was perhaps halfway across the hall when the lights went out, and she stayed there until they were on again.

"I don't suppose any of you can produce witnesses to back up your stories," Butts snapped.

After a moment of silence, Tess cleared her throat. "I can't speak for the others, but I was worried about Mary and, as I was trying to get to the booth, I called her name. She answered from some distance away. Of course, I can't say exactly where she was."

"I think there was a woman sitting at the admission table who might have seen me," Marlene said hesitantly.

"It was probably Hilda Murdoch," Mary said.

Butts made a note. "I'll talk to her."

Nobody else could think of anyone who might substantiate their stories. Butts thrust out his square jaw. "The way I figure it, the killer didn't hang around that booth after he'd killed the woman. He got away in the dark. So none of your alibis holds water, far as I'm concerned. They're holey as sieves, in fact. At this point, you're all suspects. So keep yourselves available for a couple of days."

Rex Brindle bristled. "Now see here—"

Butts's head swung around on his thick neck. "No, you see here, Mr. Seamstress—"

"Seamstress!" Rex cried. "I am a quilt artist, sir!"

Butts gave him a sinister grin. "Whatever. By the way, how did you and Cassie Terhune get along?"

"Fine," Rex snapped.

Tess glanced at him sharply, wondering if she should speak up. But Marlene Oxley saved her the trouble. "Forgive me, Rex, but I must say that you and Cassie quarreled only last night."

If looks could kill, Marlene would have drawn her last breath on the spot. "Thanks a lot," Rex growled.

Butts's thick brows shot up. "Quarreled? What about?"

"She stole some of my designs," Rex said huffily. "I merely informed her of my intention to pursue legal action against her."

This caused a murmuring in the ranks, which Butts quelled by glaring at them.

"Tell you what, Mr. Quilt Artist," Butts said sarcastically. "You hang around when I've dismissed the others. I want to know exactly what passed between you and Cassie Terhune." Leaning forward, he planted his hands on his hamhock thighs. "How about the rest of you? Anybody else had a beef with the victim lately?"

When nobody spoke, Rex said defiantly, "I heard Julian Hyde say that if Cassie thought he was going to stand by and let her bankrupt him, she had another think coming."

"She was going to bankrupt you?" Butts asked Julian Hyde.

Rex answered for him, "Cassie was publishing her own books instead of letting the Hydes' company do it, and she was about to launch a quilt magazine which would have been in direct competition with the Hydes' publication."

"Oh?" Butts stared at the Hydes. Phyllis, hanging on to her husband's arm, darted a furious glare at Rex, then looked suddenly vulnerable and frightened.

"That," blustered Julian, "is absurd. Rex, you know I abhor violence. I wouldn't hurt a fly."

"You saying you didn't threaten Cassie Terhune?" demanded Butts.

"No, I did not. I may have said I wouldn't let her bankrupt us, but that's a far cry from threatening to harm her physically."

"Mebbe," Butts said, "but it sure looks like some of you so-called friends of Cassie Terhune didn't like her much."

Nobody would meet the chief's eyes.

Butts heaved a put-upon sigh. "Anybody else got something they want to tell me? Now's the time to spill it." Nobody spoke.

Tess thought of the conversation she'd overheard between Cassie and Letitia Lattimore, but you couldn't call that a quarrel, thanks to Letitia. She decided to say nothing about it for the moment.

"How many of you knew where the circuit box was?" Butts asked.

"I did," Luke said quickly. "As a member of the chamber board, I came by here regularly when the exhibition hall was under construction. I was here the day they were putting in the breakers."

Butts made a note and looked up. "Who else?"

"I noticed the box yesterday," Tess admitted, "when I

was helping Mary arrange the quilt guild's booth.''

Butts shook his head, as if to say he should have known, and made another note. "What about you, Miz Franks? Did you know where the box was?''

Mary, whose face was still paler than normal, shook her head. "I was too intent on what I was doing, I guess.''

Tess shifted impatiently. If the killer was there, he wasn't likely to admit to knowing where the circuit breakers were.

"Anybody else?'' Butts queried. Nobody spoke. "So who turned the lights back on?''

When the lights came back on, Tess had seen the man, recognized his face as somebody she'd noticed before around town, but she couldn't name him. Finally, Kendra Lawson said in a frightened little voice, "It was Mr. Dundee. I've seen him at football games. His son's on the team.''

"That would be Carl Dundee,'' Butts said. "I'll have a talk with him.''

Tess thought that would be futile. She was almost certain neither Mary nor Cassie had known Carl Dundee and, therefore, he could have had nothing to do with the murder.

Tess touched Mary's arm to get her attention and whispered, "Do you know Dundee?'' Mary shook her head. Deep in Mary's eyes, Tess saw fear flickering, which made her wonder if Mary had begun to accept the possibility that she was the killer's intended victim, that she was alive at that very moment by a mere quirk of fate.

Neill, who'd been standing at attention beside the chief's chair, his hands behind his back, bent down to say, "The murder weapon was wiped clean, Chief—''

Butts turned blazing eyes on the young officer. "Whyn't you just broadcast it, Neill?''

Neill turned red. "Sorry, Chief. I—I was just gonna ask if you want me to dust the breaker switches for prints, too.''

"That sounds like a real good idea, Neill,'' Butts snarled,

his voice dripping with sarcasm. When Neill hesitated uncertainly, Butts barked, "Get the lead out, man!"

"Yes, sir!" Neill scurried off.

Tess knew the police had to be thorough, but if the killer had the presence of mind to wipe the murder weapon clean, he would not have touched the breaker switches with his bare fingers, either.

"OK," Butts said, "you Hydes wait around with Mr. Brindle, while I talk to Miz Patterson and Miz Franks and the girls. The rest of you can go on about your business—for now. Oh, except you"—Butts pointed a thick finger at Tess. "I wanta talk to you again in a minute." He waved at the Drunkard's Path booth. "And nobody sets foot in that booth till Neill here has gone over it thoroughly."

Letitia and Marlene left the hall for the concession area. Rex slid down a wall and sat on the floor, glowering, his arms around his drawn up knees. The Hydes walked away a few steps and began to converse in whispers. Luke remained at Tess's side, his jaw set as if daring the chief to tell him to leave the hall. Butts looked at Luke for a moment, then decided not to make an issue of it.

"Miz Patterson," Butts said in an accusatory tone, "your booth was on one side of the crime scene and the home ec booth, where Miranda and Kendra were, was on the other. You didn't speak up when I asked if anybody heard anything in there. It's hard to believe somebody got killed a few feet away from the three of you and nobody heard a thing."

Miranda and Kendra glanced at each other and then at Sandra, who said, "I heard a lot of things. People were talking, some of them were yelling. And a few people were moving around in their booths or trying to get back to their booth—like Mary."

Mary nodded. "As I told you, I'd gone to the rest room and was coming back when the lights went out. After that,

I may have progressed a few more yards by touching booths as I moved. But I was still a good distance away when the lights came on.''

Neill returned from the breaker box. Butts looked at him sharply. Neill shrugged and lifted one finger. Evidently there was one print on the breakers, which would probably turn out to belong to Carl Dundee who'd restored light to the hall. Like the murder weapon, the breakers had surely been wiped clean by the killer.

Butts's gaze returned to Sandra Patterson. "You should have heard the murderer—his footsteps, at least."

Sandra hesitated. "Moments after the lights went out, I thought I heard a movement in front of my booth, like somebody stopped for a second and then went on."

Butts's eyes narrowed. "Any idea who it was?"

"No," said Sandra regretfully. "Not by name, anyway." She paused, reluctant to continue. She exchanged a look with Tess before she added, "It could have been the killer, reaching out and taking a rotary cutter from a basket of them that was sitting on my counter."

"Rotary cutter?" Butts looked blank for an instant, then his expression shifted. "Is that what you call that thing that was used to cut her throat?"

Sandra admitted that it was.

"Vicious-looking tool," Butts observed. "One good swipe across her gullet, and she was dead meat. A little more force, and he'd have beheaded her."

Kendra mumbled, "Oh, gross," and covered her mouth with her hand. As for Miranda, she was looking green.

"You can't tell me any more than that?" Butts demanded of Sandra.

"I wish I could." Sandra sighed. "But that's all I heard, and I barely heard that."

"You girls," Butts barked, "what did you hear?"

"We heard the partition fall," Kendra said.

"Didn't you hear that?" Butts bristled, glaring at Sandra Patterson again.

"Yes, I heard something fall close by. I didn't know what it was or where. I'm sorry. I thought you meant Cassie or the killer. I should have mentioned the partition."

Butts waved Sandra's apology away. "It's clear from the crime scene that the victim grabbed hold of a quilt and pulled it and the partition down on her as she fell. You girls should have heard the killer's footsteps right before and right after that partition fell."

"But we didn't!" Miranda insisted.

Butts looked skeptical. "Think about it. Maybe you'll remember."

"We already did," Kendra said. "We didn't hear anything but that one loud crash."

"Maybe the killer wore soft-soled shoes," Sandra suggested.

"Or slipped his shoes off to commit the murder, then put them back on again when he was clear of the booth," Tess said.

"Thanks for the brilliant insights, ladies," Butts muttered. While Andy Neill examined every inch of the Drunkard's Path booth, Butts questioned the Hydes and Rex Brindle again about their differences with Cassie Terhune. Basically, the three told the same stories they'd told earlier. Finally, Butts dismissed them, along with Sandra Patterson, Kendra, and Miranda. Then he turned to Mary Franks.

"I want to know all about this close call I heard you had this afternoon."

"You mean the boards falling from the loft?"

"You had any other close calls today?" Butts asked irritably.

Mary's pale face flushed pink. "No, but the boards— that could have been just an accident. There's no guard rail or anything to keep them from falling." Plainly, Mary wanted desperately to believe that.

"They couldn't have fallen without help," Tess inserted.

"I'll get to you in a minute," Butts yelped. "Till then, shut up!"

With a warning scowl for Butts, Luke put a protective arm around Tess, who clamped her mouth closed and boiled in silence.

"Now, Miz Franks, get on with what happened," Butts said. "I'll decide if it was an accident or not. And I don't need any help from amateur snoops. I know how to do my job."

Tess groaned softly, for Luke's ears only.

Mary related the incident in few words.

Butts studied her speculatively. "Sounds like you're lucky to be alive. If you hadn't run when you did . . ."

"I suddenly had a feeling that I was in danger," Mary said.

"A premonition, right," Butts said, disgruntled, and glanced at Tess. "Seems to be a lot of that going around. You know of anybody who'd want to hurt you, Miz Franks?"

Mary winced and shook her head. "No one."

With a sigh, Butts reached for his crutches, positioned one in each hand, and struggled to his feet.

"Chief," Tess spoke up. "Can we clean up the booth now?"

Butts looked around at Neill, who said, "I'm through in there."

"It's all yours," Butts mumbled and stumped out.

Tess saw him stop and speak to Marlene for a few minutes. When she was sure Butts had left the building, Tess said, "Luke, would you mind staying here for a minute. I want to talk to Marlene Oxley."

She found Marlene and Letitia having coffee in the concession area. Tess sat down on the bench, facing them across the redwood picnic table. "Are you two all right?"

"We will be," Letitia said, "once we get over the shock."

Marlene nodded grimly.

"I admit Cassie wasn't my favorite person," Letitia went on, "but I wouldn't wish what happened to her on my worst enemy."

Tess wondered who Letitia's worst enemy might be, but said instead, "Letitia, I couldn't help overhearing you and Cassie in the guest parlor yesterday."

Letitia's eyebrows rose fractionally. "Oh?" She was probably wondering if Tess eavesdropped on all her guests' conversations.

Tess squirmed uncomfortably. "It was quite by accident, I assure you. Cassie was saying something about the choice of colors for your quilts being unsophisticated."

Letitia's cheeks flushed pink, and her jaw hardened. "That was just Cassie being Cassie. I was used to her little digs."

Marlene looked pained. "It was Cassie's way of making herself feel important," she said sadly. "I know she appeared self-confident, but underneath her brash, aggressive exterior, she was pretty insecure."

Letitia looked at Marlene in surprise. "Really? I never would have suspected Cassie had any doubts about herself at all."

Marlene nodded. "She compensated by criticizing others. Last night at dinner, she went on and on about Mary."

"What about Mary?" Tess asked.

"Cassie thought she'd had more than enough time to get over her husband's suicide. She said she was sick of Mary's moping around about it, that it was time she got a life."

"Sounds just like Cassie," Letitia muttered.

"We were supposed to go to Mary's for dinner this evening," Marlene continued, "and Cassie wanted to get out of it." Marlene's mouth drooped. "I guess she got that wish, didn't she?" She paused and stared down at the table for a moment, undoubtedly seeing Cassie's bloody corpse. Finally, she swallowed and looked up. "I told her if she didn't go to Mary's, it would hurt Mary deeply. She finally said she'd go, but she wasn't going to stay any longer than she had to. She must have realized later that she was being too hard on Mary."

"Why do you say that?" Tess asked.

"Because today she insisted Mary go and lie down. She even took over the booth for her." Marlene halted and swallowed hard.

"That *was* pretty out of character for Cassie," Letitia mused.

"Only the people who knew Cassie well realized how insecure she was," Marlene said. "Getting divorced didn't help, either. Cassie always said that it was her choice, but my husband and I know Ralph, and I've gotten the idea that he's the one who wanted out of the marriage. Cassie would never admit it, though."

Letitia studied Marlene reflectively. "I thought you and Cassie were close friends."

"We were, but I wasn't blind to her faults. I'd known her for years. I'd learned to accept her as she was."

"She must have been desperately unsure of her own abilities to steal Rex's designs—if that's what happened," Letitia said.

Marlene nodded glumly.

"Marlene," Tess said, "I saw Chief Butts talking to you before he left . . ."

"He wanted to know if Cassie was married. I told him about the divorce, but he still wanted to get in touch with Ralph. I told him Ralph works for the Cooper Truck Company in Kansas City."

Tess thought for a moment. "I've been thinking about what you told Chief Butts before that, Marlene."

Marlene looked at her sharply. "I told him the truth."

"I'm not suggesting that you didn't," Tess said hastily. "But you are the only one who might have caught a glimpse of the killer."

Marlene was shaking her head. "Why do you say that? I saw nothing. I have no idea who could have hated Cassie so much."

Tess didn't bother saying that it might have been Mary Franks whom the killer hated. Butts had ridiculed her theory. He might have said he'd follow up on it just to appease her, when actually he intended to do no such thing. So she'd follow up on it herself—quietly.

"What I meant was that you passed through the door to the concession area right before the lights went out," Tess explained. "That happens to be the one place in the hall with a view of the circuit box."

"Well, I didn't know that. I never even noticed the circuit box. And I certainly didn't see anyone near it."

"Are you sure?" Tess persisted. "You could have caught a movement from the corner of your eye and dismissed it."

"I didn't see a thing," Marlene insisted. "I was going for drinks for me and Cassie. That's all that was on my mind."

Tess sighed. "Will you just think about it? You might recall *something*."

"I won't," Marlene said stubbornly. "And I don't like the tone of your questions. I didn't even look that way. I saw nothing, I tell you."

Chapter 9

Tess left Marlene and Letitia in the concession area and returned to the Drunkard's Path booth to find Mary and Luke there.

"I'd better call and check on my repairman," Luke said. A few minutes later, he returned to report that the repairman had relayed an urgent message from one of Luke's clients. "I have to return to the office," he said, "I'll come back if I can. Are you going to be all right?"

"Don't worry about me," Tess told him. "We'll handle things here." She kissed him good-bye.

Mary glanced at the darkening stain on the floor, where it had soaked through the quilt, and shuddered. "I think I'm going to be sick!" she wailed and ran for the rest room.

While she was gone, Tess found a rag, wet it at the drinking fountain in the concession area, and cleaned Cassie Terhune's blood from the floor. She did it mechanically, trying not to think about the fact that it came from a woman who, less than an hour ago, had been alive and well. Then she took down the raffle sign and put away the blank raffle tickets. The Drunkard's Path quilt would probably remain in the custody of the police for some time. Even if it was returned soon, Tess doubted they would ever get the stain of Cassie's blood out of it. Perhaps they could find another quilt for the raffle, but until then they could sell no more tickets. Tess wondered distractedly how difficult it would be if they had to return the money they'd already collected. But that was an insignificant worry beside the others that circled through her mind.

The police had been gone for half an hour, and the crowd had dwindled. Some of the people who'd been in the hall before had left on the heels of the police, their interest in browsing through the booths extinguished by the murder. Others were venturing back inside, but so far they were avoiding the Drunkard's Path booth, the scene of the crime.

Mary had found two guild members to be in charge of selling admission tickets for the rest of the afternoon so she wouldn't have to deal with that for the rest of the day, at least. Tess wondered if she should go back to the rest room and check on Mary. As she was trying to decide, Miranda and Kendra drifted over to the Drunkard's Path booth.

"Will you watch our booth for us while we get a Coke?" Miranda asked.

"Sure," Tess said. "In fact, it would be a good idea if the two of you went home for the rest of the day."

Miranda shook her head. "We're OK. Where's Mother?"

Clearly the girl wanted to stay because she was worried about her mother. "She went to the rest room," Tess said, deciding not to mention that Mary wasn't feeling well. She didn't want to add to Miranda's worries. "You girls go ahead and take your break," Tess went on, "and take your time. I can watch both booths. It's not as if we're rushed off our feet right now."

"Yeah, really," Kendra mumbled as the two girls left.

A moment later, Mary returned. Her face no longer had that sickly greenish tinge. Now it looked as though she was wearing one of those liquid facial masks that turned stiff after it was applied.

Tess took one look at her and stated flatly, "You should go home."

Mary risked a second's glance at the floor where the stain had been. Seeing that the blood was gone, she straightened her shoulders with an obvious effort. "Why do you keep trying to get rid of me?" The words trembled on the edge of tears.

"Oh, Mary, that's not it. I'm worried about you."

She drew in a shaky breath, seemed to gain control of herself. "I'll be fine. Really. I'd rather stay here, keep busy."

"Whatever you want." What else could Tess say? Mary was too emotionally overwrought to be reasonable, but arguing with her would surely bring on a torrent of tears. Tess resolved to drop the subject but keep an eye on Mary.

The muffled drone of voices from other areas of the hall was the only sound for several moments. Tess had seen some folding chairs leaning against the wall earlier. Now she got two and brought them back to the booth.

Mary sank into one. "Thanks, Tess." She blew out a deep, indrawn breath, chewed her bottom lip for an instant, and finally asked, "Does that policeman even know what he's doing?"

"Butts? Yes, I'd say he usually does," Tess replied. "Even though he may lack finesse and his methods may be a bit unorthodox."

Mary raked tangled brown hair out of her face. "He was so cranky," she said. "Maybe he was in pain—from his leg."

Tess sat down in the second chair. Elbow resting on the counter, chin in hand, she kept a surreptitious eye on Mary, whose irritation—directed at Butts for lack of a better target—might turn to sobs at any moment. It was natural that she was taking Cassie's death harder than anybody, expect perhaps for Marlene Oxley. The three had been friends for years. But Tess was discovering a streak of stubbornness in Mary that she hadn't seen before. Though she was clearly unnerved, Mary adamantly refused to go home. Well, perhaps she was right. Maybe it would be worse for her to be alone.

"Being cranky and insulting is Butts's usual modus operandi," Tess went on. "Luke says he's got a chip on his shoulder because of his upbringing. His father was an alcoholic, and they were desperately poor."

Mary leaned forward, resting her forearms on the counter. She stared at her clasped hands. "A lot of people were raised in poverty," she said, looking up. Her eyes glittered with moisture. "It didn't make them mad at the world. The man must be in his forties. It's time he got over it."

Odd, Cassie had said something similar about Mary's continuing grief for the loss of her husband. But then Tess guessed the suicide of one's husband would be one of the hardest things to overcome. And now she had to deal with the murder of an old friend, too.

"You're right about Butts," Tess said.

Suddenly, Mary winced. "You're probably thinking I'm one to talk. My friends say I've had time to get over losing Gerald, and I know they're right, but sometimes . . . well, it's hard."

"I understand," Tess said.

Mary took a gulp of air, steadying herself. "I wonder . . . oh, dear, I just thought of something." At least, Tess told herself, the rigid mask had shifted, and Mary grimaced, as if with pain. "Ralph Terhune, Cassie's ex-husband should be notified of what's happened."

"Butts is going to call him," Tess told her.

Mary expelled a breath. "That's good."

"I didn't know she was divorced, until Marlene mentioned it a few minutes ago."

Mary nodded regretfully. "Five or six months ago, I think. I don't know what happened, but Marlene said the divorce was bitter. Still, they were married for more than twenty years. Gerald and I used to spend a lot of time with Cassie and Ralph and the Oxleys." She looked at Tess helplessly. "I'm so glad the police are going to notify Ralph about Cassie. I just don't think I could tell him."

"Did the Terhunes have any children?"

"No." Mary shook her head sadly. "But Cassie's mother may still be living. Ralph would know, and he'll know how to reach her. I'm sure he'll want to call her, anyway, once he learns about Cassie." All at once, her face seemed to crumple, and she pulled a tissue from her skirt pocket and wiped her eyes. Her hand trembled. "I don't understand, Tess—for someone to kill her, and in such an ugly, violent way," she said brokenly. "Cassie wasn't always diplomatic in dealing with other people, but she didn't deserve . . ." She swallowed a sob and pressed the tissue to her eyes. After a moment, she murmured, "She was one of my oldest friends, and I'll miss her."

Earlier, Tess had thought that Mary realized that *she* might have been the intended victim. Now Mary didn't sound as though she had.

Mary must be forced to face the possibility so that she could be on guard, but Tess didn't think this was the best time to mention it. Instead she asked, "Did Miranda say anything about her lunch with Shannon Diamond?"

Mary seemed relieved to have her mind diverted from the murder. She balled the tissue in her hand. "She and Kendra enjoyed it immensely. It's very thoughtful of Shannon to pay so much attention to them."

"Don't you think it's odd, Shannon inviting them to lunch?"

"Odd?" She looked bewildered. "I never thought about it. It's unusual, I guess." She reflected for a moment. "But then Shannon seems to be an unusual young woman. Most people her age are pretty self-absorbed, but Shannon is so interested in other people—of all ages."

"I'm not sure that's entirely accurate," Tess mused. "It seems to be you and Miranda she's interested in. Did you know she questioned Gertie Bogart about you and your late husband?"

"Gertie?" Mary was obviously mystified. "That's *weird*, Tess."

"Gertie thought so."

"What sort of questions did she ask?"

"How long you'd lived here. Where you lived before that. What your husband looked like."

"Of all the—" Mary sputtered, caught between curiosity and indignation. "You know, now that I think about it, Shannon mentioned Gerald to me, too. She said how sorry she was that I'd lost him. But then she wanted to know how and where we met and how long we'd been married. I told her it would have been twenty-three years next January. I said it didn't seem possible it had been that long. Shannon commented that she'd been barely two years old when we married, so to her it seemed like forever. I thought maybe she was trying to be helpful by getting me to talk about it."

"That could be," Tess admitted, "but every time I see Shannon with you or Miranda, I get a wild suspicion that you two are the real reason she's in Victoria Springs."

Alarm sharpened Mary's gaze. "But that's impossible, Tess. She didn't know us before she came here."

"Are you absolutely sure about that?"

"Of course, I'm sure!" Mary's emotions were still ragged, Tess realized, sorry she'd put Mary on the defensive.

Unintentionally, but all the same . . . "Don't you think I'd remember if I'd met her before?"

"I didn't mean that . . ." Tess shook her head helplessly. "Oh, I'm not sure what I mean. Is it possible she knew your husband?"

Mary stiffened. "If you're suggesting Gerald had an affair with that—that child . . ."

"I'm suggesting no such thing," Tess said hastily.

"Well, don't even think it. Gerald was totally devoted to me and Miranda."

Then why did he commit suicide and leave the two of you to fend for yourselves? Tess wondered. But perhaps he *was* thinking of Mary and Miranda when he chose suicide rather than prison. He must have known that either would be devastating for his family, but death was, at least, quick and final. She could understand how someone who wasn't thinking clearly could see it as the honorable way out.

Tess thought it time to steer the conversation in another direction. "Naturally, Shannon's attention is flattering to Miranda," she said, "but could it be that Shannon wants to spend time with Miranda in order to question her, too?"

Mary chewed the inside of her cheek and thought about Tess's words. "It still makes no sense," she said finally, "but I'll certainly ask Miranda what went on at lunch. I'll wait until this evening, when I can talk to her alone." She pressed the tips of her fingers together, and when she looked at Tess again, her eyes held a stricken expression. "I don't understand anything that's happening to me lately, Tess. Those boards falling . . ." She sucked in a breath. "Why did you tell Chief Butts that you think somebody pushed them off the loft?"

Unfortunately, it appeared that Tess would not be allowed to postpone this conversation, after all. "Because I'm convinced it's true," she said gently. "When we went up to the loft yesterday for the partitions, I noticed that those two-by-fours were stacked a safe distance from the edge. You mentioned that yourself, right after they fell practically on top of you, remember? I went up to the loft again and looked around. Two of the boards were still there, and they were a good five or six feet back from the edge of the loft, just as I remembered. Do you see any way they could have moved themselves across the floor and over the edge of the loft?''

Mary hugged herself, rocking slightly back and forth on the chair. ''No,'' she murmured at last, ''but nobody was up there. I would have seen them come down the stairs. I couldn't have missed them. Unless—'' She shivered. ''Unless there's another way out.''

''There's an outside staircase,'' Tess said, ''and the door to that staircase was unlocked.''

Mary hugged herself tighter. ''You're sure?''

''Yes.''

''You're trying to make me believe the boards were pushed, aren't you, Tess?''

''I don't think you should dismiss the possibility,'' Tess said cautiously.

Mary was silent for a long moment. ''It could have been kids, fooling around with the boards. It probably scared them when the boards fell, so they ran away.''

Tess let several more moments pass before she asked quietly, ''Do you really believe that, Mary?''

Mary abruptly pushed herself off the chair and stood, as if she had to put some distance between herself and Tess's persistent questions. ''Who would want to hurt me?''

''I don't know. I thought *you* might have an idea about who.''

She shook her head adamantly, as if by doing so she could make it not true.

''It could be related to something that happened before you moved to Victoria Springs.''

Mary's eyes widened in alarm. "Why do you say that?"

"Because of the timing—during the quilt show when so many people you knew in the past are here."

Mary rubbed her eyes wearily. After a moment, she walked over to a wall hanging and straightened it, although it didn't need straightening. Then she paced restlessly to the back of the booth and halted to gaze at the blank partition where the Drunkard's Path quilt had hung. "Poor Cassie," she said thickly.

Tess said nothing.

Finally, still with her back to Tess, Mary said, "I've never harmed anybody in my life, Tess. Oh, I'm sure I've irritated people, from time to time, even angered them, but that happens in everybody's relationships."

"Of course it does."

"I've certainly done nothing to make someone want to— to hurt me." Even now, she could not bring herself to say "murder." She pressed her fingers to her right temple as though a headache throbbed there. "No more than Cassie had."

Tess knew she had to say what was on her mind in plain language, to leave Mary no way around it. "It's possible that the killer didn't mean to harm Cassie."

Mary turned abruptly from the blank partition. "What?"

"The killer may have killed the wrong person."

Something shifted in Mary's gaze and tears filled her eyes. "You're saying he—whoever pushed those boards off the loft meant—meant to kill me. And when he failed, he—" Her voice was unsteady, and she couldn't go on. But it was obvious to Tess that it wasn't the first time the thought had entered her mind. It was just the first time she'd been forced to face it head on. Tess felt like a heel, but sometimes one had to be cruel to be helpful.

"I don't have what the police would call hard evidence, Mary," Tess said gently.

Mary just looked at her, waiting.

Tess went on relentlessly, "But a murder and a near-fatal incident in the same afternoon are connected somehow."

Mary drew in a quick breath.

When she didn't speak, Tess prodded, "Do you see why I'm so worried about you?"

Mary clenched her hands. "I was supposed to be in the booth until Luke came to relieve me."

Tess nodded. "That's right, and it was pure chance that Cassie took your place. From what you told the police, you'd been gone only a few minutes. If the killer saw you in the booth, then hid somewhere—"

"Hid? But where?"

"Behind the row of booths to the left of the entrance, for example. He could have concealed himself and waited for the moment when he could approach the breaker box without being seen. If that's what happened, he wouldn't have been able to see this booth."

Mary's gaze locked with Tess's for an instant. "My God, you're right! That must have been what he did. He couldn't have seen that Cassie had replaced me. How clever of you to figure it out, Tess."

Tess shrugged. "It's the only place near the breakers where he could have stayed out of sight." She didn't like painting such a grisly picture when Mary was already upset, but Mary must be shaken firmly out of her denial, made to see that she could still be in danger. She must take precautions.

Her face pinched, Mary seemed to huddle in a corner of the booth, like a frightened animal frozen in a car's bright headlights. "You're beginning to scare me, Tess."

Better to be scared than dead, Tess thought. "I'm sorry, but I thought I should tell you why I'm so concerned. I could be wrong, of course. I hope I am."

"Did you mention any of this to Chief Butts?"

"Yes."

"What did he say?"

"You saw how Butts is. He made a sarcastic remark about my being carried away because of something I saw in a TV murder mystery, but he promised he'd keep an open mind."

Mary moved sluggishly back to the counter to lean with her elbows on it as if she needed the support. Holding her face in her hands, she stared down at the countertop. "It's just so unbelievable."

"I know. I don't understand it any better than you do."

"You won't say anything about this to Miranda, will you?"

"Certainly not. But promise you'll think about what I've said."

"I know you're trying to help, Tess, but I can't think straight about anything right now. I feel as if I'm getting hit on the head, one hammer blow after another. I'm so incredibly tired, and I'm getting another tension headache."

At the risk of sounding like a broken record, Tess said, "You should go home."

She surprised Tess by responding, "Maybe I will. I'll find Miranda and take her with me." She gave Tess a stricken look. "Oh, Tess, if I'm in danger, then she could be, too."

"I'm sure Miranda will be fine," Tess soothed.

Mary's willingness to leave, even for an hour, proved to Tess how shaken Mary was by what Tess had said. Looking wrung out and on the verge of falling apart, Mary circled the counter and left the booth.

"Mary." She halted, looked back warily. "Be careful," Tess urged. "You shouldn't be alone until the police sort this out."

Mary paused, started to say something, then changed her mind and merely nodded. She walked on.

Chapter 10

The October evening was as crisp as the pear tree's yellow leaves, which caught the light spilling from Tess's kitchen window. Beyond the pear tree, the black sky glittered with uncountable stars. Under other circumstances, Tess would long to be outside, perhaps taking a brisk walk, enjoying the celestial display and smelling the pleasant scent of wood smoke from a neighbor's chimney, rather than in her kitchen occupied with something as mundane as making a chicken-noodle casserole. But tonight she was too distracted to fully enjoy the beauties of nature.

Primrose was weaving in and out between her legs, making her wishes known with loudly insistent meows. Primrose didn't beg, she demanded. Tess's late Aunt Iris had spoiled her unmercifully, and Tess hadn't undertaken to change her, a clearly impossible task. After all, Primrose had been at Iris House first.

The cat had already been fed, but Tess was a push-over when the yellow eyes in that whiskered gray face fixed her with their imperial gaze. "OK, Miss Priss, you win." She tossed the Persian a piece of chicken. Primrose took it in her mouth and carried it to the privacy under the table, where she began to eat daintily.

Luke sat at the kitchen table, a mug of coffee in hand, blond head bent, studying the sketch Tess had made. Across the top, Tess had written, "Where Everybody Was When the Lights Went Out."

After taking down a large mixing bowl, Tess stirred together cooked noodles, English peas, pieces of cooked chicken breast, cream of chicken soup, and seasonings. It was one of the recipes she fell back on when she had failed to make out a menu and was too tired or distracted to give much thought to meal preparation.

Luke glanced up. "This helps fix the scene in my mind, but I'm not sure it provides any clues to the killer."

Tess emptied the contents of the mixing bowl into a buttered casserole dish. "All I had to go on was what they told Chief Butts, but we know the killer was at the circuit box when the lights went out. So at least one of them has to be lying."

"Provided one of these people is the killer."

Was Luke trying to poke holes in her theory? Probably he was just being logical. "Provided, yes," Tess agreed, crumbling buttered whole-wheat bread crumbs over the top of the casserole.

Luke mulled it over. "It almost has to be one of them," he conceded, "*if* Cassie Terhune was the intended victim— but I thought you were of the opinion that Mary Franks was the target."

Bending down, Tess slid the casserole into the oven. She straighened and, gazing out the window, watched a star fall. Another death, she thought morosely.

She turned around. "Even then, Luke. If the killer was somebody Mary knows in Victoria Springs, he wouldn't have committed the murder at the quilt show, with dozens of people around. He'd have had time to plan and carry it out elsewhere."

"That makes sense. Doing it somewhere else, without

witnesses, would have been far safer. He ran a big risk that somebody would see him at the circuit box.''

"True." Tess was pleased that Luke was coming around to her point of view. "And that indicates to me that he had to do it while the quilt show was going on because he's leaving when it's over." She moved to the refrigerator and got out fresh spinach, mushrooms, tomatoes, celery, and carrots. After lining the vegetables up on the counter, she started making a salad.

"He or she," Luke amended, in his precise semanticist mode.

"Yes."

Luke stared into the depths of his coffee mug before lifting it thoughtfully. Tess studied his clean, masculine profile as he drank.

"So," he said, "you think it was someone Mary knew before she moved here."

Returning to chopping celery, Tess nodded. "I hope Butts keeps his word to investigate Mary's background as well as Cassie's for potential suspects. Another thing—" Distracted by a new thought, she reached for a plump tomato. She diced the tomato, thinking about Shannon Diamond's questioning of Mary Franks. Where had Mary lived before coming to Victoria Springs? How long had she and Gerald been married? What had Gerald looked like? Weird questions to ask a stranger.

And what had Shannon and Miranda talked about at lunch? Perhaps Mary would tell her tomorrow. Probably it still would make no sense to Tess. Nothing about the occurrences of the last two days did. She watched Luke drain his mug.

"What other thing?" Luke prompted.

"I'm wondering if I should have told Butts about Shannon Diamond's unusual interest in Mary Franks."

He set the mug down abruptly. "Oh, come on, Tess. You

don't really think Shannon Diamond is the killer, do you?''

Tess's frown deepened. ''I admit it's hard to imagine it.'' Frankly, it was hard to imagine anyone named in her crude drawing as a murderer, either. ''All I know is that something's going on with that young woman.''

He glanced back at Tess's sketch. ''She's not on the diagram.''

''Because she wasn't questioned by Butts. She only met both Cassie and Mary this week—or so everybody keeps telling me. Mary swears she'd never laid eyes on Shannon before yesterday.''

''Then it's true. Mary wouldn't lie about it.''

''Oh, I'm sure Mary didn't lie. If she'd known Shannon before and had any doubts about her, she wouldn't have encouraged Miranda to go off with Shannon for lunch.''

Luke stared at the map. Primrose, who had finished eating the piece of chicken, moved close to Luke's feet, sat with her tail curled around her back legs, and began grooming herself fastidiously.

''Oh, look, Luke. I think Primrose is being friendly. Maybe she's warming up to you.''

Luke bent to peer under the table at the cat. ''Naw. She's just pretending because she thinks I might have some chicken she can con me out of. Forget it, your highness. I'm on to you.''

Primrose looked back at Luke, her yellow eyes unblinking and inscrutable. Finally, as if realizing he wasn't going to sneak her a bite, she meowed her indifference and walked out of the kitchen, her fluffy tail held high.

''See?'' Luke said to Tess. ''That meow meant 'Screw you, buster.' ''

Tess managed a preoccupied smile. It had taken months for Aunt Iris's cat even to acknowledge Tess's existence, and she still showed no signs of making friends with Luke. Possibly Primrose was a one-person cat, she mused.

"Maybe if you brought her a treat whenever you come over . . ."

"I don't think she can be bought," Luke said.

Probably not, Tess conceded silently.

"Besides," Luke drawled, "I refuse to make all the friendly moves in this relationship. If you can call it that." He returned to studying Tess's drawing.

Tess's mind was already on other things. For a few moments, the only sound in the kitchen was the *chop-chop-chop* of Tess's paring knife. Finally, she murmured, "The first thing we have to do, Luke, is find out whatever we can about Shannon Diamond."

Luke dropped the sketch and got to his feet. She could feel his eyes on her back. He reached out, turned Tess to face him, framed her face with his hands, and tilted her head so that her eyes were forced to meet his questioning blue gaze. "What do you mean *we*?"

Impatient, she grabbed his hands and lowered them to his sides. She was in no mood for nit-picking semantics. She was incredibly tired and wanted nothing so much as to eat dinner with Luke and go to bed. But she knew she wouldn't sleep well until she'd come up with a plan to investigate Shannon Diamond.

"I assume," she said, "that you want this cleared up as much as I do. Before the killer tries again to murder Mary."

"I believe I may have said this to you before, love, but that's why we have police officers."

"There are police officers and there are police officers," Tess observed. "Unfortunately, our Desmond Butts is no Elliot Ness. Besides, he has an attitude."

Luke grinned. "I can't dispute that." He put his arms around her and pulled her close. Resting his chin lightly on top of her head, he chuckled softly. Tess could feel the faint rumble in his chest.

She moved restlessly in his arms. "What's so darned funny?"

"Something Butts said to me before we came into the exhibition hall this afternoon."

"What?"

"When I told him the victim was staying at Iris House, he said we hardly ever had any murders before you moved to town."

It was no more than Butts had said to her face, but Tess bristled, anyway. She tilted her head back to look at Luke. "That's what I mean by attitude. He can't honestly believe my presence has affected the crime rate in Victoria Springs."

"You real sure about that?" Luke teased.

"Of course I am. He just doesn't like me because I— with a lot of help from you, dear—solved that murder case last spring. Believe me, I know your help was invaluable. Why, Butts might never have figured it out if we hadn't stepped in."

He cocked his head, studying her with a meaningful smile. He knew exactly what her flattering words were in aid of. "Don't forget our involvement in the murder in June, too. It's clear as water that Butts doesn't appreciate our help."

"Tell me about it."

"Actually, he has a point, Tess. We don't have to keep sticking our noses into every murder investigation in Victoria Springs. He's being paid to do it. Cassie Terhune is Butts's problem."

"And Mary?"

"What about her?"

"I'm afraid Butts doesn't really believe the killer meant to murder Mary instead of Cassie. He could decide to ignore the idea simply because I'm the one who brought it up. I wouldn't put it past him."

"I have to say it, Tess. You're about to go off half-cocked here. Don't underestimate Butts. Besides, we don't *know* the killer murdered the wrong person."

"But suppose I'm right. Do we have to wait until he succeeds in killing Mary, too, before *that* becomes Butts's problem?"

"Tess, I'm not suggesting—"

"Good, I knew I could count on you, sweetheart," Tess said briskly. "Here's what we'll do."

The stairs creaked.

Tess struggled up from the depths of sleep, rolled over, and listened to the sound of stealthy footsteps. Somebody was coming down the stairs. She bolted upright, fumbled in the dark for her robe, and pulled it on. She checked the digital clock beside her bed. It was one fifty-five. The situation was so similar to one preceding the murder of one of her guests the previous spring, it made Tess shiver.

Without bothering to run a brush through her tousled hair or search for her house slippers, she padded quietly down the hall from her bedroom to the sitting room of her apartment.

Fumbling for the light switch just inside the door separating the sitting room from the foyer, she glanced at her reflection in the mirror beside the door. Wide brown eyes looked back at her from a pale, oval face capped by tangled auburn curls. Steadying herself, she flipped up the second switch, which lighted the foyer. At the same moment she jerked open the door. Behind her, she heard Primrose, who was curled up in her favorite chair, grumble at having her sleep interrupted.

In the foyer, Shannon Diamond, in a purple cotton-knit nightshirt with a big yellow, yawning Pluto on the front, had just reached the bottom of the stairs. She whirled toward Tess. "Oh, good grief!" Her ash-blond hair was as tousled as Tess's, and like Tess, she was barefoot. Her toe-nails were painted purple to match her nightshirt. She reminded Tess of a high school girl at a slumber party where each girl painted somebody else's toenails.

Shannon placed a hand over her heart and caught her breath. "You scared me half to death, Tess. What are you doing up at this hour?"

Tess, her hand still on the doorknob, decided she had Shannon off-guard and might as well make use of it. Shannon looked particularly small and vulnerable in that nightshirt. "Funny, I was about to ask you the same question."

Shannon yawned and rubbed her eyes. "I couldn't sleep. I guess you couldn't, either."

"I was sleeping quite well until I heard you coming down the stairs. The third and fourth steps from the top squeak."

"I woke you? Oh, I'm sorry."

"Where are you going?"

Shannon looked down at her nightshirt. "Not out on a date, if that's what you're wondering."

In no frame of mind for jokes, Tess merely waited.

Shannon sighed. "I was going to the kitchen. I'm so restless, I thought a glass of milk might help me relax."

Tess observed her curiously. At that moment, Shannon appeared to be anything but a threat. She looked more like a lost child than a successful interior decorator who might or might not have an axe to grind with Mary Franks. And in spite of her suspicions about Shannon's motives, Tess felt a stab of sympathy. "Something heavy on your mind?"

Shannon's face muscles all seemed to tighten at once. "Not particularly."

"Maybe it's just the unfamiliar bed."

The irony was lost on Shannon. "Probably."

"Well," Tess said briskly. "Hot chocolate might be even more relaxing than milk." In fact, Tess doubted if that were true, but she wanted an excuse to accompany Shannon to the kitchen and keep her there for a while.

"Oh, yes," Shannon agreed, unknowingly falling in with Tess's plan. "Hot chocolate would be wonderful."

Tess closed the apartment door and turned on the lights in the guest parlor. Their bare feet padded softly across the hunter green carpet as they passed skirted rose and green chintz chairs, a sofa, and a green velvet settee. A wide archway led from the parlor to the dining room with its latticework ceiling; heavy, dark carved fireplace mantel, sideboard, and buffet; and colorful sea-green and raspberry needlepoint rug. The large oval table, surrounded by Windsor chairs, was placed near a window through which guests had a view of the south side yard and gardens while they ate breakfast.

They entered the kitchen. To keep the Victorian look of the modern kitchen as authentic as possible, the bulbs were cleverly recessed from sight around the edges of a pressed tin ceiling. They lit the room warmly—glass-fronted white cabinets, airy lace curtains, and brick-colored ceramic tile floor. Tess had been so pleased with the kitchen remodeling that she'd had the builder create a smaller version of it in her apartment.

Tess got out a saucepan, milk, and the jar containing the hot chocolate mix that Gertie kept in the cabinet to the right of the range. She measured two cups of milk into the saucepan, added several spoonfuls of the mix, and turned on the burner.

Shannon pulled out a chair and sat down at the round oak table with a heavy sigh. Winding her legs around the chair's legs, she cupped her chin in her hand.

October nights were chilly but, because of two furnace vents beneath the cabinets, the tile floor was warm under Tess's bare feet. Stirring the chocolate, Tess watched Shannon stare at the star-spangled blackness beyond the large window next to the table. But Tess didn't think Shannon was marveling at the beauty of the Ozark autumn night. In fact, she sensed that Shannon was hardly aware of what she was looking at; whatever she was focused on was in her mind.

"What a terrible day this has been," Tess mused as she filled two mugs with steaming chocolate.

"One I won't forget for a long time," Shannon agreed.

"I suppose Chief Butts questioned you about where you were when the lights went out," Tess ventured.

Shannon blinked and turned her gaze from the window. "What did you say, Tess?"

If only Tess could read minds. She was sure it would be enlightening to know what was so absorbing to Shannon that she couldn't sleep and hadn't even heard Tess's remark. "I was just saying that Chief Butts must have badgered you about where you were when the lights went out in the exhibition hall."

"No. Why would he do that?"

Tess managed a nonchalant shrug. "I just assumed he had, since he asked everybody else who's staying at Iris House that question. I'm sure he'll get around to you eventually."

"But I hardly knew Cassie Terhune. I hadn't even heard of her before I got here."

"Really?" Tess set both mugs on the table and pulled out a chair.

"Uh-huh," Shannon responded, testing the chocolate cautiously with the tip of her tongue.

"I thought, since quilts are an important part of country decor, you'd probably done business with Cassie. She's very well known in the quilt world."

Shannon scowled. "Well, I never even heard of the woman before I arrived in Victoria Springs. Why are you giving me the third degree, Tess?"

"Oh, I'm sorry." My, aren't we prickly? Tess thought. "I didn't mean to be intrusive." But she couldn't help thinking that an interior decorator should have heard of the best-known quilter in the country. She blew on her chocolate and took a tiny sip, giving Shannon what she hoped was a disarming smile.

"It so happens," Shannon said, her blue-green eyes suddenly shrewd, "that I was in the rest room when the lights went out."

Tess tried to detect more clues in Shannon's expression. What was she thinking? Tess couldn't pick up the tiniest hint. "That's where Mary Franks was. She went there to lie down for a few minutes. She'd just started back to the guild's booth when the lights went out."

Something flickered in Shannon's eyes. "Well, she wasn't there when I went in." Was that glint caused by the mere mention of Mary's name? Or was Shannon making up her alibi as she went along and now realized that Tess might be able to check it out?

Tess suspected that Shannon was lying. If she was in the rest room when the lights went out, she'd have seen Mary leaving or crossed paths with her en route.

There was only one reason for Shannon to lie—she was unwilling to divulge where she really was when the lights went out. And why should she be unwilling? Because she was at the circuit box?

That's where Tess's suspicions hit a brick wall.

As far as Tess knew, Shannon had no motive to kill either Cassie or Mary. Tess, in fact, was completely bumfuzzled by Shannon. But she felt an urgency to get behind Shannon's facade. "You must have just missed Mary then," she said dismissively.

"Probably." Shannon took a swallow of chocolate, set the cup down. Her face was a blank mask now.

"Did you enjoy your lunch with Miranda and Kendra?"

"Sure. Miranda—well, both of them actually—are good kids. They remind me of me when I was that age."

"Did you grow up in Little Rock?"

She shook her head, her facial muscles relaxing now that the conversation had moved away from the murder. "No. I lived in Arbor, Texas, from when I was a few days old until I left for college. It's just a wide spot in the road. Bor—ing. I couldn't wait to get out of there."

"Are your parents still there?"

She nodded. "And happy as clams. Can you believe they wanted me to become a teacher and return to Arbor? I'm an only child . . ." She paused. "I always wanted brothers and sisters. I used to dream about belonging to a big, extended family." She sighed and the distant expression left her eyes. "But there were just the three of us. My parents want to be near their grandchildren"—she smiled slightly—"provided I ever have any."

"I'm sure you will eventually."

Shannon's sandy brows lifted. "I'm not. I'd have to feel a lot more confident than I do now that I could be a good parent."

"Why would you doubt it?"

Shannon shrugged. "Kids need roots, a sense of belonging, don't you think?"

"Yes," Tess agreed, wondering what on earth Shannon was getting at. "You had that, didn't you? I mean, you might have wanted to leave that small town, but your parents obviously loved you very much."

Shannon stared at her, her face suddenly tight. Was she angry? "You don't know anything about my parents."

It seemed Tess couldn't say anything right with Shannon in her present mood. "That's true. I just thought—well, you said they wanted you to come back home after college." Tess was bewildered to see Shannon's eyes fill with tears. Good job, Tess, she chided herself, this is the second woman you've had in tears in the last twenty-four hours. "If they didn't love you, they wouldn't care where you went."

Shannon's bottom lip quivered, making her look more like a child than ever. She stared down at her hands curled around the mug. And Tess felt sorry for her. This was a troubled young woman.

After a lengthy silence, Tess said, "I'm sorry if what I said hurt you, Shannon. That was the farthest thing from my mind."

"I know," Shannon mumbled. "It's just—sometimes I get so frustrated and depressed."

"About your parents?"

Blinking away her tears, Shannon pushed her chair back. "I'm not very good company right now, so I think I'll take my chocolate upstairs. I don't feel like talking anymore. Excuse me, please."

"Sure. I hope you can sleep now. Good night, Shannon." Nonplussed, Tess watched her leave.

Tess lingered at the table as she finished her hot chocolate. Darn, her questioning of Shannon hadn't turned up any clues—to what was bothering Shannon, the murder of Cassie Terhune, or anything else. Except that Shannon had probably lied about where she was when the lights in the exhibition hall went out.

Tess went back over everything she'd said to Shannon. It all seemed innocuous enough. Yet clearly when she'd mentioned Shannon's parents, she'd unwittingly touched a sore spot.

Chapter 11

Tess was sitting in the swing on the Iris House veranda at mid-morning the next day, when Luke pulled up in his new navy-blue Jaguar. A beautiful machine, Tess thought a bit enviously, as she mentally compared it to her five-year-old compact, which she couldn't afford to replace for at least another couple of years.

Luke waved to her as he climbed out. In navy slacks and a bulky white sweater, he looked good enough to be a male model. They would pose him leaning nonchalantly against the Jag, of course.

Unlike Luke, Tess was dressed for gardening in an old cotton shirt and a loose pair of faded khaki slacks with grass stains on the knees. Gardening gloves and a trowel lay on the floor near the swing.

She would have been amazed to know that Luke was thinking how pretty she was, even in her gardening clothes. In fact, he was thinking that he could never get enough of the slightly tilted nose with its faint sprinkle of golden freckles, the deep brown eyes, the flawless ivory complexion, the way the morning sunlight struck flashes of red in her dark auburn hair.

"Decided to take the morning off?" he asked as he bounded up the steps.

"No. I'm waiting for Aunt Dahlia," Tess told him, moving over to make room for him in the swing. "We're going to work in the iris beds."

"Oh, right. I forgot." Resting his arm along the back of the swing, he kissed the tip of her nose.

"I'm surprised you could leave your office during trading hours," she said.

"The stock market's in the doldrums, but I can check in on my car phone whenever I want. Josie is working today." Josie was the middle-aged woman who was Luke's part-time secretary. According to Luke, after Josie's initial resistance to entering the electronic age, she'd become fascinated by the stock quotations available on Luke's computer, via the Internet. "Josie kept an eye on the computer screen for me while I was on the phone to Little Rock."

According to the plan Tess had outlined last night, Luke was to find out what he could about Shannon since she moved to Little Rock, and Tess would see what she could learn about Shannon's life before that.

"Any luck?" Tess asked.

"Depends what you mean by luck," he said. "I talked to Shannon's boss. Said she'd applied for credit and I needed to confirm her employment. He was eager to help."

"You are so good at this, Luke. You should have been a detective."

"Flattery," he said, with a grin, "will get you anything."

She patted his knee. "So, she's really employed where she said she was."

"Yep, and the boss says she brings in more business than either of the other two decorators who've been working for him much longer. He thinks Shannon Diamond hung the moon. Said I shouldn't worry about a loan, as Shannon has a job with him as long as she wants one.''

"That doesn't surprise me. Shannon has a persistent streak that should stand her in good stead with clients.''

"Her boss also volunteered that she was out of town, searching for items for a couple of the firm's best customers. Looks like she's really here on business, as she claims.''

Tess frowned. "She's too smart to tell a flat-out lie that could be checked so easily. It doesn't mean her visit to Victoria Springs wasn't meant to serve a dual purpose.''

"Ah, Tess, you've a suspicious nature. Why have you got it in for this woman?''

"I don't have it in for her! But she's on a secret mission here, or my name's not Tess Darcy. I *feel* it, Luke. Call it a premonition, call it whatever you like.''

He held up a hand, palm out. "I believe you, honey. But whatever clandestine mission she's on, her boss is ignorant of it. And so is her landlady.''

"You talked to her landlady? How did you manage that?''

"Elementary, my dear. I told her boss I had to verify her home address, too. He gave it to me *and* volunteered the landlady's name. Said he was sure she'd give Shannon a good reference.''

"Which she did, I presume.''

"Absolutely. Shannon pays her rent on time, doesn't throw wild parties, has a sunny disposition, and she even ran errands for Mrs. Landel—that's the landlady—when she was laid up with pneumonia. She says Shannon's the best renter she ever had in her upstairs apartment. More like a daughter than her own daughter.''

Tess sighed loudly.

"Sorry," Luke said, "I did my best, but Shannon Diamond is apparently perfect.''

Tess rubbed at the grass stain on the knee of her slacks. "Nobody's perfect," she murmured. "I had an interesting conversation with Shannon last night—or this morning, I should say. She woke me coming downstairs at about two A.M. She was looking for a glass of milk to help her sleep. I made hot chocolate instead."

Luke arched an eyebrow. "And joined her for a nice, friendly chat?"

Luke knew her so well. "Of course. She was born and raised in a small town in Texas." She began counting off items on her fingers as she talked. "She hated it and couldn't wait to get away. She's an only child. Her parents wanted her to be a teacher and return to Arbor—that's where they live. I strongly suspect there's a conflict between her and her parents over something besides Shannon's choice of career. I couldn't pry any more than that out of her, but she became defensive when I said her parents obviously loved her." Tess pondered for a moment. "Maybe she thought I was taking her parents's side, even though I don't even know what the sides are. But I think it was more than that. She got very uptight, said I didn't know anything about her parents. It was as if she was thinking that if I *did* know, I'd change my tune."

He reached for her hand, which still rested on his knee. "She's right. You don't know one thing about her family."

Absently, Tess laced her fingers through his while running her free hand through her hair. "I plan to remedy that. I'm going to get in touch with Shannon's parents. I called information, and there's only one Diamond in Arbor, Texas. But no one answered when I tried the number this morning."

"You'd better come up with a good reason to talk to her parents, or they're going to be mighty suspicious. And they'll probably call Shannon and tell her somebody's asking questions about her."

Tess looked at him askance. Did he think he was the only one around here who could invent ingenious ways to elicit information? "I'll think of something." She pulled her hand from his and got to her feet. "Here comes Aunt Dahlia now. Cinny's with her."

Luke chuckled. "Cinny is going to get her hands dirty? I don't believe it."

"She may not be staying," Tess said as Dahlia's cream-colored Cadillac glided to a smooth stop behind the Jag. "Maybe her car's in the shop and she's borrowing Aunt Dahlia's."

"I have to get back to the office. Josie is leaving at noon, and there are a couple of stocks I've been watching for a client. If they drop another point, I'll buy some for his portfolio." Luke kissed her, then ambled down the front walk, stopping to say hello to Dahlia and Cinny at the curb.

"What a lovely young man," Dahlia said as she reached the veranda. She sounded just like Gertie.

As usual, every frosted hair was in place. In wrinkleless red slacks and a red-and-white polka-dot shirt, Dahlia could join Luke on the runway, modeling the "relaxing at home" look in a fashion show. She was carrying gardening gloves—red of course—a couple of tools, and a small rubber mat, presumably for kneeling on.

"He's cute, too," added Cinny, tossing long blond tresses over her shoulder. Her jeans and plaid shirt were not her usual work attire. She, too, was carrying a mat and gloves. Evidently she actually meant to help with the gardening. Curious. As Luke had observed, the spoiled only child of Dahlia and Maurice Forrest wasn't into manual labor. Cinny lived alone in her own house, but her parents' housekeeper cleaned for her, too. Tess doubted that Cinny, at twenty-five, even knew how to operate a vacuum sweeper.

"I'll tell Luke you think he's cute, Cinny," Tess said wryly.

Cinny grinned. "Fair warning, Tess. That new teacher at the high school has her eye on him."

"Luke?" Tess asked innocently.

"Of course Luke. Isn't that who we're talking about?"

"How do you know that the new high school teacher is interested in Luke?"

"She comes into the bookshop a couple of times a week. The first time, she described him *and* his car and asked who he was. Made no secret of her attraction to him. I told her he was seriously involved with my cousin." Cinny grinned impishly. "Now, every time she comes in, she asks if the two of you are still an item. We've become quite chummy, actually."

While discussing my love life, Tess thought dourly. Terrific.

"When *are* you and Luke going to announce an engagement?" Dahlia inquired. "I want to have an engagement party for you. It'll be the most elegant gathering this town has seen in ages."

"You're rushing things, Aunt Dahlia."

Dahlia ignored this. "We'll have engraved invitations, of course. Perhaps I'll have it at the country club, but I'll use that new caterer in Springfield." Dahlia never did anything by halves. "He catered Lucy Grenheldt's reception in September," Dahlia continued, "for the new pastor at the Community Church. It was stunning. The decorations were red and cream, which set off Lucy's black hair and dress. Now, for your engagement party, Tess, I think yellow—"

"Please, Aunt Dahlia," Tess pleaded. "Don't keep going on about something that hasn't even happened yet."

"Translation: It's none of your business, Mother," Cinny said.

Dahlia seemed surprised. "Nonsense. We're all family here."

Tess hastened to change the subject before Dahlia could get started on the decorations again. "Cinny, I appreciate your willingness to help, but shouldn't you be at the bookshop?"

"Notice how easily she diverts the conversation and slips right through your fingers, Mother."

Dahlia made a moue of irritation.

Cinny arched her blond brows at Tess. "I left my new assistant in charge of the bookshop. Rosalee's very dependable. A real jewel, that woman. She's never late and never asks to leave early."

Unlike her employer, Tess thought. In truth, she was quite fond of Cinny, but her fondness didn't blind her to her cousin's flaws.

"After we finish here," Dahlia said, some twenty minutes later, "that bed of Edith Whartons on the north side of the house needs thinning, too." They were digging up the Darcy Flame bed in the south side yard. The spot recalled to Tess's mind the murder victim who'd been stabbed and left there during the opening weekend of Iris House. There had been a garden tour in progress at the time. It had been such a beautiful April day, with the garden full of tourists oohing and ahhing over the irises.

And then a woman had screamed.

The lovely Darcy Flames had been stained with the victim's blood. But not as much blood as had spilled in the Drunkard's Path booth yesterday. With an effort, Tess shook off a shudder and pushed from her mind the image her memory had conjured up.

After adding fertilizer to the soil and watching how Dahlia did it, Tess and Cinny were dividing clumps of rhizomes, discarding all dead or weak-looking material, and replanting the healthy remainder.

It had quickly become clear why Cinny was there. She had been grilling Tess mercilessly about every last detail of the murder of Cassie Terhune.

Tess had related what she'd witnessed, sticking to facts and leaving out her suspicion about who the intended victim really was. Cinny would have it all over town by nightfall.

Finally, Dahlia had said, "Couldn't we talk about something a little more pleasant?" Tess could have kissed her, even though Dahlia had waited until Cinny had dragged all the information she could out of Tess.

Dahlia held up a clump of irises, examined it critically, then tossed it aside. "We have plenty of healthy plants here without saving those that are questionable," she said as she bent to dig up another clump.

Cinny straightened, shielding her eyes from the sun, and gazed toward the street. "Who's that?"

Rex Brindle got out of his car at the curb and hurried up the front walk. What was he doing there in the middle of the day? Tess caught his attention and waved.

"I'm in a hurry," he called without stopping. "I need to pick up something and get back to my booth."

"His name is Rex Brindle," Tess said as Rex disappeared from sight. "He's a well-known contemporary quilter. Or, as he prefers to be known, a quilt artist."

"Brindle," Cinny mused. "Is he the one you said argued with Cassie Terhune the day before she was murdered?"

"The same."

Dahlia had stopped digging, too. "He's certainly younger and bigger and no doubt stronger than Cassie Terhune." Dahlia had a Cassie Terhune quilt hanging on the wall in her den. She'd met Cassie and purchased the quilt at the quilt show last year. And she had apparently forgotten her request for more pleasant conversational material. "He could easily have overpowered her."

"I don't think that was necessary," Tess said. "Cassie didn't struggle or make a sound. Remember, there were people in the booths on either side of her who would have heard. And it was pitch dark, so she couldn't have seen the killer approach. Obviously, he acted before she realized what was happening."

"I don't think Brindle is the killer," Cinny announced. "It wouldn't be very clever of him to kill her only hours after he angrily accosted her and accused her of stealing his designs."

"Rex is nothing if not clever," Tess observed.

"If this were a mystery novel," Cinny pondered, "he'd be far too obvious to be the killer. It's always the person you least suspect."

"Cassie Terhune's murder is real, Cinny, not fiction," Dahlia said, attacking another clump of irises.

But Cinny would not be deterred so easily. "Who do you least suspect, Tess?"

"Cinny, please—"

"Oh, come on, tell me. Just for fun."

Dahlia frowned at her daughter. "I fail to see anything 'fun' about it."

Cinny smiled sweetly at her mother. "You know what I mean."

"OK," Tess said. Anything to shut Cinny up. "I guess the least suspicious person involved in this would be Letitia Lattimore. I simply can't envision her commiting a violent act."

Cinny's eyes lit up. "Maybe she's the one. We should investigate her, Tess."

We? Tess had no intention of bringing her flighty cousin into any investigation she undertook. "Luke thinks I should stay out of it," she said. It was the truth, as far as it went.

Looking disheartened, Cinny began gathering up discarded clumps of dead irises and throwing them into a large trash bag that Tess had provided for the purpose.

Dahlia pursed her lips. "Luke is merely trying to protect you. How sweet. And it's prudent advice."

Cinny was studying Tess. "Are you going to take it, Tess?"

"I may not have any choice."

Cinny tilted her head, her eyes narrowing. Maybe she'd realized that Tess was being evasive. Tess smiled at her and returned to her digging.

They worked for a while in silence. But Cinny's words had started Tess thinking. Letitia Lattimore was certainly an unlikely suspect in Cassie's murder. But so was Marlene Oxley. *As far as Tess knew*. And that was the real difficulty. Tess knew too little to guess who might or might not be a suspect. At the moment, Cinny was right about the *most* likely suspect—Rex Brindle was at the top of the list.

But all that was academic, if Cassie had been killed by mistake. And if Mary Franks was the killer's target, there were *no* likely suspects. Nobody involved had a reason to want her dead. That's what made the whole thing so confusing and frustrating.

There was no motive. Correction. There was always a motive; it was just that in this case it was well hidden. Tess had a feeling that if she knew the motive, she could name the murderer.

Since there had to be a motive, there had to be a way to uncover it.

But thinking evidently wasn't the way, she mused an hour later as Dahlia and Cinny left, the iris gardens now ready for a new blooming season. For the past half-hour, while companionable silence reigned in the iris beds, Tess had followed her thoughts to ridiculous extremes, and she still wasn't any closer to focusing in on a motive.

Disheartened and tired, she brushed loose dirt off her clothing and stepped into the Iris House foyer. Nedra Yates, the tall, stick-thin housekeeper who could work rings around any two younger people Tess knew, was coming down the stairs with her bucket of cleaning supplies.

"Breaking for lunch?" Tess asked.

"Yep." Nedra stepped off the bottom stair. Her gaze raked Tess's disheveled appearance, then perused her face. "Look done in," she concluded. Nedra rarely spoke in complete sentences.

"I am, but a shower will help."

"Bothered, too," Nedra added. " 'Bout that murder?"

"Yes," Tess admitted. "Cinny is trying to help, which is the last thing anybody needs. She insists on treating it like a mystery novel. For fun, I believe she said."

Nedra, a fan of mystery novels herself, snorted. Her morning's exertions had dislodged wisps of unruly hair from its pins. They stood out around her angular face, every which way, like pieces of straw.

"When I said Rex Brindle was the most likely suspect, Cinny said then of course he couldn't be the murderer."

Nedra's expression turned thoughtful. "Went in his room, came out a few minutes later."

"Rex?"

Nedra nodded impatiently, as if wondering why she so often had to say things twice. If people would only listen! "Thought I smelled something burning."

"When?"

"Didn't I just say? When that Brindle fella was here."

"Did you check his room after he left?"

Nedra shrugged. "Nope. Already cleaned it. The smoke smell went away."

Tess glanced up the stairs worriedly. "Well, I think we'd better check it now. Just to be on the safe side."

Nedra set down her bucket, followed Tess up the stairs, and used her master key to open the door of the Black Swan Room. The dark wood furniture glistened with lemon oil —

the cane side table beneath a print of the tall-bearded red-dish-black Black Swan iris, the massively scaled bed, huge bureau, and marble-topped washstand, all finished with a reddish-black lacquer. The lemon-yellow wing-backed chair and the patterned black, gray, and lemon-yellow rug were newly vacuumed. The polished oak floor, visible around the edges of the rug, shone like glass.

Tess sniffed, inhaling the faint scent of lemon oil and, yes, a hint of something recently burned. Nedra stepped into the room, sniffing loudly, and followed her nose to the black enameled wastebasket beside the washstand. She picked it up and peered inside, then handed it to Tess.

In the bottom of the wastebasket were gray ashes and a few white paper fragments that were burned around the edges. Tess picked up the only fragment on which words, written in ink, were still discernible.

Sorry and, on the next line, *make* and *pay*.

Tess handed the scorched paper scrap to Nedra. "Is it possible he came back to Iris House just to burn this?"

Nedra scowled at the paper. "Makes no sense."

Noticing a black-bound book lying on the washstand, Tess picked it up and leafed through it. It appeared to be a journal. Each page was dated. She flipped more pages until the journal fell open at a place near the back where a page had been torn out. The page before the missing page was dated two days ago. None of the pages following it had been written on.

"Looks like he burned a page from his journal," Tess said. She took the paper fragment from Nedra's fingers. "This could have said, 'She will be sorry' and 'I'll make her pay.'"

Nedra cocked her head. "Figured that out from three words?"

"You think my imagination's working overtime?"

Nedra shrugged. "Makes no sense."

"Rex accused Cassie Terhune of stealing some of his quilt designs and putting them in her new book. He could have vented his spleen by writing in his journal, after Cassie laughed in his face when he confronted her in the foyer. The next day she was killed." She pondered for a moment. "Evidently he remembered the journal entry after he got to the exhibition hall this morning, and came back to destroy it."

"Whyn't he just wait till evening?"

Tess didn't know. Maybe the entry was even more threatening than she could imagine. Maybe Rex had actually said he'd kill Cassie. If so, Tess could understand why he'd want to destroy the entry. But why make a special trip back to Iris House when he could have done it when he returned from the quilt show for the day?

"I don't know," Tess said finally. "I suppose it was worrying him."

They left the room. In the foyer, Nedra said, "Gettin' good at solving murders."

"Me?"

"Not you. Me."

"You?"

"Yep."

"In mystery novels, you mean?"

"Yep. Read more'n Cinny Forrest, I bet."

"You mean, it isn't always the least likely suspect?"

"Oh, no, that's about right. Trouble is, there's more'n one unlikely suspect."

"I see."

"Yep. You have to turn things around, look at 'em different."

Tess nodded uncertainly. Was Nedra suggesting she do that with Cassie's murder?

"For example."

"Read one last week—couldn't figure it out, till I asked myself questions."

"Such as?"

"What if this one's lying, or that one's not who he claims to be. Like that."

"I see. So you think—"

But Nedra was through talking. The conversation had been a wordy one for the housekeeper. Picking up her plastic bucket, she marched off toward the kitchen.

Chapter 12

After a shower and a sandwich lunch, Tess had to run several errands in town. She donned an aqua shirtwaist dress and a matching cardigan sweater with rose-and-white flowers embroidered down each side in front. It was an outfit that Luke particularly liked. Standing in front of her bathroom mirror, she used a brush to smooth her russet curls into a short pageboy— which would last until the first gust of wind hit her hair. She'd inherited her curly hair from her mother, who'd died when Tess was twelve. The thought was followed, as it usually was, by a pang of regret. She missed having a mother to talk to and supposed she always would. With her father, stepmother, and half-brother and sister living in France, Tess sometimes felt like an orphan. One of the reasons she'd wanted to move to Victoria Springs was that her Aunt Dahlia and cousin Cinny were there.

She gave her hair a final brush stroke and left Iris House, thinking about Mary Franks. Knowing Mary, Tess feared she would feel duty-bound to be at the quilt show all day. Tess, who had decided to try to convince her otherwise, stopped at the exhibition hall when she finished her errands.

Sandra Patterson, she noticed, had removed the

basket of rotary cutters from her booth counter. "Wish I'd put those somewhere else in the beginning," Sandra said.

"I doubt that would have stopped the murderer," Tess told her.

"That's what Chief Butts said this morning."

"Butts was here again today?"

Sandra nodded. "He'd talked to Cassie Terhune's ex-husband. I gathered Terhune said that Cassie had enemies. Butts made us all repeat what we told him yesterday. Then he took Rex Brindle outside. Rex came back fit to be tied, said he'd had to sit in a police car while Butts accused him of killing Cassie Terhune over some disagreement about quilt designs." Sandra shook her head. "Sounds pretty ridiculous to me, but Rex thought they were going to handcuff him right there. I guess the police don't have anything else to go on."

What exactly had Ralph Terhune told Butts? "So it would seem," Tess agreed. Now she knew why Rex had returned to Iris House to burn that journal entry. Butts had probably threatened to get a warrant to search his room. Tess doubted that Butts had the evidence to convince a judge to issue a warrant, but perhaps Rex hadn't thought of that. Or he just hadn't wanted to take any chances.

Tess said good-bye to Sandra and found Rose Cline, a member of the quilter's guild, in the Drunkard's Path booth. Another quilt, this one a beautiful Jacob's Ladder done in lavender, blue, and green, was displayed on the back partition where the original raffle quilt had hung.

"Hilda donated it for the raffle," Rose explained as Tess admired the new quilt. "It was in the competition. Marlene Oxley gave it second place. Maggie Dawes's Cross and Crown quilt won first."

Tess was still admiring the Jacob's Ladder quilt. "Generous of Hilda to donate a prize-winning quilt," she said.

"Really," Rose agreed. "She made this one for her married daughter. But she knows how badly the guild needs the raffle money, so she said she'd make another quilt for her daughter. The daughter doesn't know anything about it. It's going to be a surprise. So at least she won't be impatient to get it. I'm just sorry we couldn't find another Drunkard's Path fine enough to be raffled.''

"I like this one as well as the other,'' Tess said, as her mind jumped involuntarily to the image of the bloodstained quilt. She was glad the new quilt employed a different pattern and different colors. It wouldn't remind her of the one Cassie had grabbed for as she was dying.

Rose gave an impatient nod that dislodged a lock of gray hair from the knot atop her head. ''The point is,'' she emphasized, smoothing the lock back into place, ''it kind of messes up the theme of the booth, but I've sold a lot of raffle tickets today.''

"Darn, I wish I could buy a chance on it myself.''

Rose frowned slightly. ''We have an unofficial agreement among guild members not to buy chances on any quilts we raffle. If one of our members won, there are a few suspicious people who'd think the raffle was rigged.''

Tess knew that, but she only said, ''It's a good policy. I'll look around. If I see another quilt I like as well, I'll buy it to hang in the Iris House parlor.''

"If you're looking for a traditional pattern, check Letitia Lattimore's booth.''

"I intend to, but I don't have time today. Maybe tomorrow.'' Tess turned her back on the Jacob's Ladder quilt. ''Is Mary around?''

Rose's brow puckered in concern. ''She stayed at home today.''

"Well, that's a surprise.''

Rose pondered, then said, ''Mary called early this morning and asked me to take over the booth.'' She made a clicking sound with her tongue. ''That dear woman had enough grief even before one of her best friends was murdered. She said she didn't get a wink of sleep all night and she didn't think she'd be any use to anybody here.''

Tess glanced toward the home ec booth. Miranda and Kendra were occupied, talking to three women who'd entered their booth to look at the wall hangings. Tess was troubled by the thought of Mary at home alone. She'd warned her not to place herself in such a vulnerable position. Was it possible Mary wasn't taking the situation seriously enough?

"Have you seen Shannon Diamond today?" she asked Rose.

"Who?"

"Never mind. I think I'll run by Mary's house before I go home."

"I wish you would," Rose said. "Miranda told me Mary insisted that she come in and take care of the home ec booth today. Said she was needed here more than at home. But on the phone, Mary sounded"—she paused as though searching for the right word—"like she was at her wit's end. Frazzled. You know what I mean?"

Yes, Tess knew. Mary would have to be at the end of her emotional rope to turn her duties at the quilt show over to somebody else. Working with her the past few weeks, Tess had learned that Mary was one of those people who had trouble delegating. She couldn't stop worrying if she wasn't in control.

Tess went back to her car and drove to the Franks's house on Elm Avenue. It was a square structure with gray vinyl siding and white shutters in a neighborhood of well-cared-for homes built in the last ten or twelve years. An oak tree was shedding yellow and orange leaves across the lawn. The yard looked like one of Mary's appliqued quilts, bright leaves on a green background.

Tess had been to the Franks's home several times since

she'd volunteered to help Mary at the quilt show. From the front, the house looked like a simple one-story, deceptively small. A living room and dining room separated by a wide, oak-floored foyer faced the street, but the lot sloped down sharply, and in back, the house contained two stories with three spacious bedrooms on the lower level, plus a second living area and a big, beamed country kitchen on the upper level.

Most single mothers would not be able to afford such a house, especially one who didn't earn a salary. Mary's only occupation, besides caring for her home and her daughter, was quilting, but that was more for her own enjoyment than for income. Mary had told Tess once that, even though she'd been unable to collect on her husband's life insurance—because of the suicide verdict—Gerald Franks had left a large brokerage account in Mary's name. Evidently that money had been made before the insider trading incident and the exposure of the ill-gotten fortune he'd had to return.

Standing in the brick-paved outside entryway, Tess rang the bell three times before Mary came to the door in a white terry robe. Her face was flushed and there were dark smudges beneath her eyes. "Oh, it's you, Tess. Sorry to keep you waiting. I was soaking in a hot tub."

"Then I'm the one who's sorry," Tess said, "for disturbing you."

"No, it's all right. Come on in."

One of Mary's creations, a Lone Star wall quilt, hung in the entryway. Tess followed her back to the big, bright kitchen, where a wall of windows looked out on a garden area and bricked patio with white wicker furniture. A stone fireplace and bookshelves covered one wall, an appliqued Ohio Rose quilt hung on another wall.

"My stomach feels tied in knots," Mary said, "I thought a hot bath might help me to relax." She went to a counter where an automatic coffeemaker sat, its red light glowing. "I made a fresh pot of decaf. Would you like a cup?"

"Yes, please."

While Mary got down two gray pottery mugs, filled them, and arranged a tray with cream and sugar, Tess wandered over to a window and watched a yellow tabby trying to creep up on a wren. The cat, whose name was Maxwell, was Miranda's. Maxwell succeeded in progressing to within three feet of the bird before it took flight. The cat sulked off and crawled beneath a bush to wait for other prey.

Glad that the wren had escaped, Tess turned away. She was standing next to a small round lamp table with a maple-framed love seat beside it. A drawer in the lamp table was pulled out halfway. Light reflected off a piece of glass inside the drawer. Looking closer, Tess saw that the glass, which was broken, covered a photograph in a wood frame. The picture appeared to be a snapshot that had been enlarged for framing and showed three couples in casual attire. All six smiled up at Tess from the drawer.

It was a moment before she recognized the three women: Mary Franks, Marlene Oxley, and Cassie Terhune. They'd been at least ten years younger then, maybe fifteen years younger. The three men had to be Mary's, Marlene's, and Cassie's husbands, and it was easy to identify which was which, as each man had his arm around the woman next to him. Cassie Terhune's husband was stocky with thick dark hair, Marlene Oxley's was tall and thin—he could have passed for Marlene's brother. Gerald Franks had been a burly, handsome man with flaxen hair and a wide smile.

Tess stared at the faces. The way Marlene's mouth turned up at one corner struck a familiar chord in Tess's memory, but then she'd probably seen Marlene smile like that in the last few days.

The snapshot had been taken long before Cassie's divorce and Gerald Franks's suicide. Six happy people in happier times. Perhaps Mary had put the picture away until she could get the glass replaced. Or perhaps the memories evoked by the smiling faces had become too much for her, so she stuck the picture in the nearest drawer, out of sight.

Tess nudged the drawer closed. She felt a little guilty, as though she'd been observing people through a bedroom window.

Turning away, she smiled at Mary as she came from the kitchen, carrying the tray. They sat in cane-bottomed chairs at the maple drop-leaf table. "I went by the exhibition hall," Tess said. "Rose told me you'd decided to take the day off."

Mary gave her a wan look. "I couldn't sleep last night. I kept seeing Cassie—" She swallowed and, after a moment, went on. "This morning, I almost bit Miranda's head off when she insisted she should stay at home with me and leave Kendra to handle the home ec booth alone. Between you and me, Kendra is a little flighty. Anyway, I finally convinced Miranda I'd be better off here by myself. I didn't want to subject anybody to my cranky company today."

"I don't like your being alone, Mary."

"I'll be all right. I have a good security system."

Tess could see that arguing with her would be useless. "I hope you can get a nap."

"I have a pill I can take if necessary. I needed them for a while after—after Gerald died."

"You should take one and lie down," Tess said.

Mary summoned a feeble smile. "I will, a little later. I think I was in shock yesterday. It was only after I got in bed last night that it really hit me." She added cream to her coffee, took a sip, and looked out at the garden where bronze and yellow chrysanthemums were in bloom. After a moment, she glanced back at Tess. "Did the police get in touch with Ralph Terhune?"

Tess nodded. "I heard that Chief Butts talked to him."

Winding a strand of kinky brown hair around her finger, Mary took a deep breath. "This has to be rough for him. They may be divorced, but they were deeply in love once."

"What happened?"

Looking down, Mary gripped her mug in both hands. "I don't know. Cassie was never one to confide in her friends."

"Well, don't worry about Ralph Terhune."

Mary took a swallow of coffee. "Right. I have other things to worry about."

"Forget the quilt show for today, too. Rose Cline is quite capable of taking charge."

Mary's look was almost apologetic. "I hope so because I wouldn't be much help there today. Anyway, I had another reason for staying home besides lack of sleep. I don't want to run into Shannon Diamond."

Tess felt a tiny stirring of alarm. "Has she come by the house?"

"No, but she phoned here last night while Miranda and I were having dinner. Our number is unlisted, you know, but she got it from Miranda yesterday at lunch. When she asked Miranda for the number, Miranda didn't think twice about telling her. I probably wouldn't have, either, at the time."

Tess thought Shannon had taken advantage of Miranda, who'd probably been flattered by the attention of an adult. "What did Shannon want?"

"To know how I was feeling." Mary shook her head. "It was nice of her, but I just can't cope with another problem right now. The things you said yesterday, Tess, made me start to question Shannon's motives. She's beginning to make me feel uncomfortable."

And frightened, too, Tess guessed, which had probably contributed to Mary's inability to sleep last night.

"Mary, did you see Shannon anywhere shortly before the lights went out in the exhibition hall?"

Mary thought about it. "No. Why?"

"Shannon told me she was in the rest room the whole time the hall was in darkness."

Mary frowned. "Well, I suppose she could have been . . ."

"But you came out of the rest room and had started back to the Drunkard's Path booth when the lights went out, yet you didn't see Shannon."

Mary caught her breath. "I see what you're getting at. Since she wasn't in the rest room when I left, we should have passed each other in the hall. Unless Shannon took another route . . ."

"The only other route I can think of is to go behind that partition Snodgrass put up next to the stairs. I guess she could have done that," Tess said doubtfully, "but it's not the most direct route."

"I'm sure I don't know what she did." Mary pressed two fingers to her temple. "But then I don't understand anything about Shannon. She's an enigma." She dropped her hand. "Maybe we did pass each other and I just didn't see her. I wasn't feeling well, you'll remember."

"Maybe," Tess mused, "but Shannon could also be lying."

"She could be, but I can't think why."

Tess didn't voice the thought that flashed briefly across her mind. Shannon might have been at the circuit box. The idea seemed less outlandish than before. If it occurred to Mary, she kept it to herself.

"I can't figure out where she's coming from," Mary went on. "Even Miranda is beginning to wonder. Shannon quizzed her endlessly at lunch yesterday."

"About what?"

"Me, mostly."

Tess looked at her sharply, yet she wasn't surprised. "Really?"

Mary scowled gloomily. "She wanted to know where I went to high school. Where I went to college. What my maiden name was. How long I'd known Gerald before we married." A confused expression settled on her drawn face. "That's all I can remember right now, but it was just more of the same." She pondered for a long moment, then looked close to tears. "Why *is* that girl so obsessed with my past?"

"I wish I knew." A glimmer of an idea niggled at Tess, but it wasn't solid enough to wrap her mind around yet.

"Could she be truly insane, yet able to appear normal to others? Do you think she's fixated on me for some crazy reason and is stalking me?"

"No, I don't think so, but she is definitely troubled." Tess told Mary about her middle-of-the-night conversation with Shannon.

"She actually cried?"

"She didn't boo-hoo, but her eyes filled with tears," Tess clarified. "That's when she excused herself and went upstairs."

And that morning at breakfast, Shannon had hardly said a word to the other guests. She was obviously preoccupied, though she had eaten a healthy portion of Gertie's scrambled eggs and ham-and-cheese biscuits before leaving the table to go to her room. Where she remained until she departed Iris House at nine-thirty, presumably for the quilt show. Shannon must have been disappointed to discover that Mary wasn't there.

"I'd hate to have to ask Shannon to stay away from Miranda, but it may come to that—if she keeps quizzing Miranda." Mary shrugged helplessly.

Tess's heart went out to her. Shannon was deliberately adding more stress to Mary's already burdened emotions.

"Do you think I should tell Miranda to avoid her, Tess?" Tess hesitated. "She'd want to know why."

"Mmm, and I don't have a reason, just a vague nervous feeling."

"It occurred to me that we might find out what Shannon's up to from her family," Tess said. "I've been trying to reach Shannon's parents, but they aren't answering their phone. I'll keep trying."

"What will you say to them?"

"I don't know yet. And they may not tell me much that'll help us understand what's going on here. I would guess, from what Shannon said, that they're very protective of her. But we need to know what's on her mind, and contacting her parents is the only starting place I can think of."

"They may not know anything about this—whatever it is."

"That's a possibility. I gather Shannon hasn't lived with them for seven or eight years, since she went away to college." Tess reflected for several moments.

Mary shifted in her chair. "Maybe you could get in touch with one of Shannon's high school teachers. At least you could find out what Shannon was like as a teenager—if she had emotional problems, for example."

"It's worth a try, I guess," Tess said, "but I'll keep calling her parents' number for a day or two first."

"Thank you for wanting to help, Tess. I know you have more than enough to do at Iris House."

Tess didn't say she was beginning to fear that Shannon's presence in Victoria Springs was related somehow to the murder. Not that she had any real evidence of a connection. It could be pure coincidence. But it bothered Tess, and she wouldn't be able to lay her fear to rest until she knew why Shannon was asking so many questions about Mary.

"Please don't be concerned about me, Tess," Mary was saying. "I'm quite safe here. I keep the doors locked, and I'll turn my security alarm back on when you leave."

"Good. And don't open the door to anyone you don't trust."

Mary's eyes narrowed worriedly. "To Shannon, you mean?"

"If I were in your place, I wouldn't. At least, not if I was alone."

"All right. It's better to be safe than sorry."

Or dead, Tess thought.

"But I can't imagine that Shannon means me any physical harm."

There were more kinds of harm than physical, Tess mused, and immediately wondered what kind of emotional or mental harm Shannon could inflict on Mary, other than the irritation of her persistent questions.

As Tess drove toward Iris House, she thought of Nedra's advice. Turn things around. Look at things in a different way. OK. Assume Shannon's interest in Mary was not connected to Mary's "accidents" or Cassie's death. What else could she be up to? Blackmail? Extortion? Revenge? Each seemed more unlikely than the previous idea. What had Mary ever done that somebody could blackmail her for? As for extortion, that would require superior physical force or knowledge that Mary didn't want made public, neither of which seemed to apply in this case. And revenge? Since Mary hadn't known Shannon until two days ago, there was nothing for Shannon to seek revenge for.

Nedra's advice didn't help at all.

Back in her apartment, Tess wondered if Shannon was in her room. Maybe she should confront her, ask her point blank why she was nosing about into Mary's life. But she'd tried getting information from Shannon last night without much luck.

In desperation, she dialed Shannon's parents' number in Arbor, Texas again. The phone rang four times and Tess was ready to disconnect when somebody answered.

"Hello." It was a woman, and she sounded out of breath.

"I'm sorry to disturb you—"

"It's all right. I've been out." She paused long enough to catch a breath. "Heard the phone ringing when I got out of the car. I'm expecting a call, so I ran to catch it. Who is this?"

"I'm a friend of your daughter, Shannon."

"You live in Little Rock?" Fortunately, she didn't wait for Tess's answer. "Then maybe you can tell me why Shannon hasn't called her parents in two months. She's put one of those answering machines on her phone, and I've left a dozen messages. She's not returning my calls."

"I don't know anything about that, Mrs. Diamond. I can't imagine Shannon acting that way."

"She never used to. Till she got that crazy idea in her head . . . well, I'm sure you know what I'm talking about, you being Shannon's friend."

"Mmm," Tess said, hoping Mrs. Diamond would keep talking until Tess got a hint.

"She claims she's thought about it for years, but she never acted any different until last summer. Came to stay a week, but when we refused to help her, she got mad and left after two days."

"But you've talked to her since then surely."

"*I've* talked, sure. Phoned her once a week, like I always did before. Shannon's end of the conversation consisted of one-word replies. Then she got that machine so she wouldn't have to talk to me at all."

"Shannon told me you wanted her to move back home."

There was a silence on the other end of the line. "We'd like to see her more often, but that's not what this is about." Her tone was guarded now. "Listen, lady, I don't even know who you are. What did you say your name was again?''

Tess hung up.

Well, that was no help. She paced restlessly around her sitting room. Primrose, who was lying in a patch of sunlight on the carpet, stretched lazily, rolled over on her back in case somebody took a notion to scratch her stomach, and watched Tess pace.

What next? Tess asked herself. Finding a teacher who would talk about Shannon didn't seem very promising, but she'd try tomorrow if she hadn't come up with a better plan by then. She looked at her watch. It was too late to find anybody but possibly a janitor at the high school in Arbor today.

Tess wandered around the sitting room a few times before flopping on the couch. Primrose leaped up to join her, curling up beside Tess and nosing Tess's hand. Still pondering her conversation with Mrs. Diamond, Tess scratched between Primrose's ears. The cat settled more comfortably against Tess and began to purr loudly.

Tess sighed. It was so frustrating to feel the need to *do* something, but have no earthly idea what. OK, she asked herself, what had she learned from the conversation with Mrs. Diamond?

She made a mental list. Shannon was so angry at her parents that she wasn't returning her mother's phone calls. Shannon had gone to Arbor last summer, intending to stay a week, but had left after two days when her parents refused to help her.

Help her what? Buy a house, go into business for herself, go back to school . . .

Tess groaned. It could be almost anything.

Chapter 13

Fifteen minutes later, having given up trying to dig any sensible meaning out of what Mrs. Diamond had said, Tess acted on an impulse. Even though it was a little after five, she dialed information and got the number of the Cooper Truck Company in Kansas City. Before she could talk herself out of it, she dialed the number and asked for Ralph Terhune.

"Let me see if he's still in," said the woman who answered.

Tess was still trying to formulate what she'd say to the man when he came on the line.

"Ralph Terhune here."

"Oh—Mr. Terhune," Tess stammered. "This is Tess Darcy. I own the bed and breakfast in Victoria Springs, Missouri, where Cassie was staying when . . . er, I just wanted to say how very sorry I am."

"Thank you," he said tonelessly.

Tess waited, but he offered nothing more. "I was wondering what I should do with Cassie's things."

After a pause, he said, "I hadn't even thought about that, what with talking to her mother and helping with the funeral arrangements. Cassie's body will be shipped here in a day or two . . ." He trailed off.

149

"If you'll give me her mother's address, I'll ship Cassie's things to her."

"No," he said quickly, "don't do that. It'll just upset her all over again. Send them to me." He gave Tess his address.

"I'll take care of it. We're all still in a state of shock here over what happened. You don't expect ordinary people to be . . . er, murdered."

"How well did you know Cassie, Miss Darey?"

"Not very well. I'd only known her a few days."

He hesitated as though to weigh his words. "Cassie was different than she seemed." He paused, took a breath, then added in a rush, "She used people, and when things turned out badly, she did whatever she had to do to keep herself out of trouble."

"I don't understand—"

"I'm sorry, but I have to hang up. I've said too much already, and I have another call waiting." He disconnected before Tess could try to stop him.

What had he meant? What had turned out badly? And what had Cassie done to "keep herself out of trouble"? If only she could have kept him on the line longer . . .

Frowning in frustration, she left her apartment and peeked into the guest parlor to see if any of her guests were there. She'd heard the stairs squeak a few minutes ago, but whoever it was must have been going up instead of down. The parlor was empty, but beyond the parlor and dining room, Gertie stood in the kitchen doorway, hands on her wide hips, a look of bewildered consternation on her round face. As usual, Gertie wore a flowered tent dress and a bibbed white apron. Ordinarily she'd have gone home by this time in the afternoon.

"Hi, Tess," Gertie said abstractedly.

Tess went back to the kitchen. "Still here? Don't you have things to do at home?"

"Nothing pressing. My husband will be late, so I was going through my recipes, planning menus for next week."

"Has Nedra left?"

Gertie nodded and turned to the work station in the center of the big kitchen. A recipe card file sat on the counter with a stool drawn up to it.

"I'm pulling out recipes I haven't used in a while," Gertie said.

"For that cookbook you're working on?"

"No, I finished that. It's at the print shop right now. It's got all my favorite recipes. I'm going to sell it at the Christmas bazaar all the churches in town put on."

"Save a copy for me."

Gertie nodded. "Just now I was looking through my file for something new for breakfast. Found some recipes I haven't used in years. Kind of got caught up in it—until Shannon Diamond interrupted me."

Shannon again. "What did she want?"

"Marched right in here and asked for directions to Mary Franks's house."

"Good grief. That woman is relentless. I was with Mary less than an hour ago. She needs to be left alone today. She has to rest."

Gertie shook her head. "Taking Cassie Terhune's death real hard, is she?"

"Yes, and she doesn't need anything more to trouble her. Shannon's behavior is beginning to frighten Mary."

"Don't blame her. Shannon went to the quilt show this morning looking for Mary. Found out Mary stayed home today. I don't know what Shannon was doing the rest of the day, but when she came back here, she told me Mary was trying to avoid her."

"She actually said that?"

"She sure did. Acted like it made her mad, too. Like she thought Mary had some kind of obligation to entertain her or something." Gertie sighed heavily and sat down on the stool, smoothing her apron down over her ample lap. "She got downright huffy when I said I was feeling uncomfortable because of all I'd already told her about Mary. When I wouldn't tell her where Mary lives, she right near blew a gasket. Got a temper, that girl has."

"Where did she go?"

"Back upstairs, I reckon."

"I'll have a word with her," Tess said, "explain that Mary needs to be left alone."

"Lots of luck." Gertie snorted. "Shannon Diamond's got a determined streak a mile wide. She let something slip—made me think she's been making calls to Kansas City, asking questions about Mary and her late husband. If that girl wants to find Mary, I got a feeling she'll find her."

Tess felt her own determined streak hardening. "We'll see about that." She turned abruptly and hurried back through dining room, parlor, and foyer, and up the stairs to the Carnaby Room.

Shannon answered Tess's knock with a cross "Who is it?"

"Tess. May I speak to you a minute, Shannon?"

She opened the door wide enough for Tess to step inside. Behind Shannon lay an expanse of rose-red carpet and a white-canopied bed Shannon's purse lay on a rose velvet chair, its shoulder strap hanging to the floor, its contents spilling out on the cushion, as if she'd thrown it down with considerable force when she came back to the room. The phone book lay open on the bed.

"I've just talked to Gertie," Tess said.

"Message central, huh?" grumbled Shannon.

"She told me you were asking about Mary Franks again."

Shannon shrugged indifferently.

"Gertie said you went to the quilt show looking for Mary."

Shannon crossed her arms and looked belligerent. "I had business to conduct at the quilt show,"

"You were also looking for Mary," Tess reiterated.

"So what if I was!" Shannon snapped.

"She stayed at home today."

"Thanks for the hot news flash, Tess, but I already knew that."

Tess was beyond being insulted by this woman. She gestured at the phone book. "If you're looking for her number, I think it's unlisted."

"So the operator told me," Shannon said sourly. "Anyway, I have the phone number. What I want is her address."

"I don't think you should go there, Shannon."

Shannon scowled at her. "Oh, is that so? What are you, Mary Franks's keeper?"

"Merely her friend. And she's really not up to having company today—especially you."

"What is that supposed to mean?"

"Shannon, the way you're going around quizzing everybody about Mary, it's frightening her."

"Oh, really? I suppose she told you that."

"Not in so many words, but the way you're behaving, you've got Mary and Miranda both a little worried. If she finds out you've been calling Kansas City, asking people she knew questions . . ."

"Great. I suppose your faithful cook told you that, too."

Tess did not respond.

"OK, so I talked to a former business associate of Gerald Franks. He didn't tell me anything I didn't already know. Franks killed himself because he was about to be indicted for insider trading in the stock market. It's public knowledge, anyway."

"I can't imagine why you'd be interested in that."

Shannon shrugged again. The blue-green eyes fixed on Tess were challenging.

Tess tried once more. "Mary asked me if I thought you were stalking her."

"Stalking!" Shannon snorted. "That's ridiculous."

"What else is she to think? Why are you so interested in Mary?"

"Why don't you ask her?"

Tess almost ground her teeth. Sometimes talking to Shannon was like running in circles. "I have. She has no idea what you want."

"Of course she'd say that."

"Are you saying she *does* know?"

"What I'm saying is she's a lot dumber than I think she is if she hasn't figured it out by now. That's why she's avoiding me all of a sudden. But she can't avoid me forever. Mary Franks is going to look me in the eye and explain . . ." Shannon halted abruptly.

Tess waited, but Shannon had clamped her lips together and didn't go on. "Explain what?"

Shannon shook her head. "I'll let Mary tell you if she wants you to know—after I've talked to her."

"Then you're determined—"

"I'm sorry, Tess, but I have things to do. This is none of your business. You'll have to excuse me."

Tess ignored the blunt dismissal. Shannon had gone from being a house guest to be pampered to being the harasser of a friend. "I spoke to Mary about an hour ago. She's not feeling well. She was going to take a sleeping pill and go to bed."

Shannon stared at her truculently. There were dark smudges beneath her lower eyelids, and the faintly wild look in her eyes intensified Tess's worry. "Is this a story you and Mary cooked up so I'd leave her alone?"

Tess finally lost patience. "Oh, for heaven sakes, Shannon. Mary has a right to her privacy. If you keep this up, she could report it to the police."

"Let her. I can talk to her at the police station as well as anywhere." Shannon's lack of concern about the police surprised and confused Tess. "But I will talk to her, Tess. Sooner or later." She spun on her heel, walked to the bathroom, opened the door. "Good-bye. Be sure the door locks behind you."

The bathroom door clicked shut in Tess's face.

Tess stood still, staring at the door in total frustration. She tried to make some sense out of Shannon's bizarre fixation. Shannon seemed to think that Mary knew full well why Shannon was asking questions about her, yet Tess would swear that Mary had no idea. But whatever the reason, real or imagined, it was obviously of vital importance to Shannon.

The sound of the toilet flushing made Tess jump. She turned quickly and headed for the door. As she reached to open it, her glance fell on the contents of Shannon's purse that were strewn over the rose chair cushion. A tube of lipstick, compact, ballpoint pen, small address book, and a folded sheet of paper—a document of some sort.

Tess opened the door while trying to read the section of the document that was visible.

Baby girl . . . unnamed

Father's name, unknown

Reaching out, Tess pulled the document toward her far enough to read another line: *mother's name, Mary Lane.*

"I thought you'd gone."

Tess jerked her head around. Shannon had come out of the bathroom so quietly she hadn't heard her. "I'm . . . uh, just leaving," Tess said and scurried out, pulling the door firmly shut behind her.

For a moment, she leaned back against the door, her

heart pounding. A birth certificate? Shannon had a birth certificate in her purse. Her own? It must be. She wouldn't be carrying around the record of some other female child's birth. An unnamed child. Father unknown. Mother's name, Mary Lane.

What was Mary Franks's maiden name? That was one of the questions Shannon had asked Miranda. A light went on in Tess's brain.

She sucked in a deep breath and hurried down the stairs and into her apartment. She was ashamed of snooping in Shannon's things, but glad to have finally found a piece of the puzzle.

After several minutes thinking it through, there was only one conclusion Tess could reach from this. It now seemed clear to Tess what Shannon was after. But Tess needed more proof than a glimpse at an unidentified document. She could, after all, be wildly off the mark.

Primrose, who was asleep in her favorite chair, awoke and lifted her head as Tess entered the sitting room. "Hi, lazybones," Tess greeted her absently.

The cat jumped down and meowed loudly.

"Time for your dinner. I know."

Primrose followed her to the kitchen and wound herself around Tess's legs as Tess opened a can of cat food and emptied it into Primrose's dish. Leaving the cat to eat, Tess returned to the sitting room.

One thing was obvious. She had to talk to Mary again before Shannon got to her. She had to warn Mary.

Still, she hesitated. She would really like to know first if her suspicion was valid. If so, wouldn't Mary have guessed who Shannon was by now? Perhaps she knew but was pretending not to know, hoping to discourage Shannon. In any case, Tess didn't want to ask Mary point-blank, not if there was any other way.

She stared at the telephone. Whom could she call? She

couldn't phone the high school in Arbor, Texas, until tomorrow morning, and she wasn't likely to find out what she wanted to know there, anyway. Then who else might help her?

She went to the secretary and opened a drawer, took out the scrap of paper on which she'd written Shannon's parents' phone number. She rested her hand on the telephone. The worst that could happen was that they'd tell her to mind her own business.

Taking a deep breath, she lifted the receiver and began to dial. This was probably futile, she told herself as she listened to the first ring. Mrs. Diamond hadn't told her anything earlier. What reason would Shannon's mother have to reveal more now, especially after Tess had refused to identify herself and hung up on the woman? No reason. It was just that she had to do something, and she couldn't think of anything else at the moment.

She'd apologize for hanging up before, say she needed information because ... Tess's mind went blank. She couldn't think of a single plausible excuse for wanting information about Shannon.

But now, at least, she had an idea why Shannon had wanted help from her parents and why they had refused.

"Hello."

The man's voice startled Tess. Shannon's father? "Is this Mr. Diamond?"

"Yes."

"I'm sorry to bother you, sir, but I'm ... uh, well, I'm worried about Shannon."

"Who is this?"

"I'm a friend of Shannon's. Something's going on with her. She's not herself, Mr. Diamond." The words spilled out. Tess didn't want to give him opportunity to ask another question, such as her name. "She's taken time off work and gone to Missouri with that birth certificate. I guess you know about the birth certificate.''

"The original one?'' He sounded depressed. ''Yes, she showed it to us. We didn't think she could get it, you know, but that search group she got involved with knows all kinds of tricks. I can't believe there's not a law to stop those people snooping around in other peoples' business.''

"I wouldn't know about that, but Shannon was pretty upset that you wouldn't help her.''

"We couldn't. We didn't know the name of her birth parents or anything about them. Shannon wouldn't believe us. The thing is, we don't understand why she'd want to find the woman who gave her away. This is killing her mother . . .'' He paused, and Tess heard his sharp intake of breath. ''Her *real* mother,'' he went on, his tone harsh as if daring anybody to disagree, ''the mother who raised her since she was four days old and we brought her home from that little clinic outside Kansas City.''

It was true then. The Diamonds had adopted Shannon, and Shannon was searching for her birth mother whose name was Mary. Somehow she had tracked her to Victoria Springs.

Finally, Shannon's questions made sense. Tess didn't feel particularly cheered by having her suspicion confirmed.

"I'm sorry,'' Tess said. ''I'll tell Shannon you want her to call you.''

"Please. We've left messages on her answering machine, but since she's not there, she may not have gotten them.''

The poor man clearly wanted to believe that, but according to Mrs. Diamond, she had been leaving Shannon messages for two months.

"You say she's not herself?'' he asked, reluctant to let Tess go. He believed Tess was a link to his daughter.

"What I meant was that she's obsessed with this search. She seems to think she's found her mother in Missouri now.

Maybe if this woman really is her mother and they can talk—well, maybe Shannon will be satisfied. I'm sure Shannon will get in touch with you soon, Mr. Diamond. Try not to worry about her.''

Tess cradled the receiver. She wanted desperately to go back to the Franks's house immediately. But Mary had said she was going to take a sleeping pill, and she needed the rest. Tess would go there first thing tomorrow morning, then. Before Mary left for the quilt show. Before Shannon confronted her.

The last thing Mary needed was to find out who Shannon was at the exhibition hall with all those people around. Tess realized that she had virtually accepted that Mary was Shannon's birth mother. It could be a mistake, but Shannon, at least, was convinced that her search had ended. She'd asked Miranda what her mother's maiden name was, and she'd evidently learned it was Mary Lane. Otherwise, Shannon would have realized she'd made a mistake.

Barring some bizarre coincidence, Mary Franks was Shannon's birth mother. Tess paused to examine the thought. Oh, dear. There could be very good reasons for Mary's having given up a baby. She might even welcome the chance to meet that baby as an adult—at the right time. But there couldn't be a worse time for Mary to come face to face with the daughter she gave up for adoption.

Mary would have been nineteen or twenty when Shannon was born twenty-five years ago, and Mary had said she'd married Gerald Franks less than twenty-three years ago. Since Mary had refused to name the father on the birth certificate, he may not have been Gerald Franks.

Now Shannon was going to demand to know why her mother gave her up and who her father was. How would Mary react?

Shannon was angry and felt she had a right to know these things. Surely Mary had already guessed what Shannon was after. And if Mary told her, would Shannon insist on telling Miranda that she was her sister?

Tess sighed. How much more could Mary take right now?

Later, when she was sure Miranda was home, Tess phoned the Franks's house.

"Is your mother sleeping?" Tess asked.

"Yeah. She was asleep when I got home."

"Good. She needed it."

"Well—I don't think I should wake her."

"I agree," Tess said quickly. "I'll just leave a message."

"Just a sec. I need like a pencil. OK, got it."

"Tell Mary that I'll be at your house at eight-thirty tomorrow morning. I have to talk to her before she leaves for the quilt show. It's important."

"OK, sure. I'll tell her."

"And, Miranda—"

"Yeah?"

Tess didn't want to frighten the girl. "If somebody else calls for Mary—or comes by the house—please put them off. Don't bother your mother this evening."

"Like who do you think will come by?"

"Nobody in particular. I just know how much your mother needs her rest right now."

"OK, sure."

Tess took a deep, steadying breath as she hung up. At least she'd diverted Shannon until tomorrow.

But if Shannon *did* try to talk to Mary tonight and Miranda got in the way, Shannon wasn't likely to blurt out the whole story to the girl. Surely Shannon had more compassion than that. The story would have to come from Mary. Shannon must be made to understand that.

But Shannon was angry, blaming her birth mother for giving her away, blaming her adoptive parents for refusing to help her search. The anger had probably been festering for years. Angry people were often immune to reason and common sense. Fueled by that anger, Shannon might behave in ways that she would regret in a more objective mood.

Suddenly Tess's thoughts frightened her. Just how angry *was* Shannon? Angry enough to act out in a violent way?

Was she angry enough to want to kill the woman who gave her up for adoption?

Angry enough to plan and carry out a murder that went terribly wrong?

Chapter 14

All of Tess's guests were at breakfast the next morning before she appeared. Her night's sleep had been fitful, broken by periods of anxious worrying about what the day would bring for Mary Franks and Miranda. She'd spent an extra few minutes on makeup, which she usually gave short shift. But she'd needed it today to camouflage the circles under her eyes.

She always had breakfast with her guests, made an effort to get to know them and to make sure they were enjoying their stay. "Good morning," Tess said.

They replied in a chorus, all except Shannon, who was munching on a strip of bacon and didn't bother looking up.

Gertie came out of the kitchen carrying a plate of her sour cream waffles. "Seconds, anyone?"

"Here," Justin Hyde caroled, drawing a disapproving look from his wife.

Gertie ladled a waffle onto his plate and another on the plate at the head of the table for Tess. "Anybody else?"

"I'm stuffed," Marlene Oxley said. In a beige cotton dress, she looked particularly washed out, making Tess think that Marlene could have used a little extra

162

makeup herself today. "Justin," Marlene went on, "how can you eat another one?"

"He's got a bottomless pit for a stomach," said Phyllis, grimacing as she watched her husband add butter, strawberries, and whipped cream to his waffle. "And he never gains a pound."

Justin gave Marlene an exaggerated grin, smoothed his mustache, and batted his eyes.

Letitia studied Justin's plate with envy. "Disgusting, isn't it?"

"Indeed," agreed Phyllis.

Tess took her seat, scanning the bowls of fruit on the table strawberries, blueberries, and blackberries. After buttering her waffle, she spooned on blackberries and added a sprinkle of powdered sugar and a dollop of whipped cream.

Gertie poured coffee for Tess, then replenished cups around the table before returning to the kitchen.

Glancing up, Shannon caught Tess's eye, then frowned and looked away. She's still put out over my advice that she leave Mary Franks alone, Tess surmised. Now that she knew why Shannon wanted to talk to Mary, Tess was sure Shannon had no intention of heeding her advice.

At Tess's right hand, Marlene Oxley was sipping her coffee, head bent slightly. In addition to looking pale, Marlene appeared tired. Tess guessed that Cassie's murder was keeping Marlene, as well as Mary Franks, awake. What were the police doing, Tess asked herself, besides checking suspects' backgrounds? Had their checks uncovered any new evidence? Rex had been the last of them to be questioned, so it didn't appear that there was new evidence to follow up on. Was it possible that Ralph Terhune had told Chief Butts more about Cassie and the way she used people than Terhune had revealed to Tess? If so, Butts wasn't about to share it with Tess. She only hoped, whatever information Butts had, it would be enough for him to arrest Cassie's murderer quickly.

Watching Marlene, who was gazing abstractedly out the window at two robins flitting along the top of the wrought-iron fence, Tess reflected that it would be even more difficult for Cassie's friends to put the murder behind them if it was never solved. Marlene and Mary had gone to school together, and it suddenly occurred to Tess that if Mary had had an illegitimate baby twenty-five years ago, Marlene could well know about it. If the untenable happened and Shannon barged into Mary's life at this, the worst possible time, Marlene could be a support for her friend.

"I spoke to Cassie's ex-husband last night," Marlene said. "They're having a private burial service Sunday afternoon—for family members only. I suggested a memorial service later for Cassie's friends. It's going to be next Thursday morning at ten. I'll know more details later. I hope you all can make it."

"We'll try," said Phyllis, with an uncertain glance at her husband.

"I can't be there," Rex said flatly.

"As far as I know, I can," Letitia put in.

Looking down the table, Tess let her gaze rest on Letitia for a moment. She wore a blue cotton dress, and her hair was done up in a twist on top of her head. Her eyes were bright and clear, her cheeks a healthy pink, her expression expectant. Plainly Letitia, for one, was having no trouble sleeping.

"You look bright-eyed and bushy-tailed this morning, Letitia," Tess observed.

A smile wreathed Letitia's face. Tess had the feeling Letitia had been waiting for somebody to remark upon her upbeat demeanor. "I have some good news and I simply can't keep it to myself any longer."

All eyes turned toward her. "Pray tell us," Rex Brindle grumbled. "I could use some good news."

"Poor, mistreated Rex," murmured Phyllis insincerely.

"At least you haven't been arrested," Justin remarked. "I take it you were able to satisfy the police chief yesterday that you aren't a murderer."

Rex shot him a scathing look. "That imbecile wouldn't know a murderer if he was coming after him with an axe."

Phyllis repressed a smile. Justin chuckled. Marlene's lips turned up on one corner in a slight smile, but she looked uncomfortable. As for Shannon, who had ladled a spoonful of strawberries onto her plate and was eating them slowly, one by one, she appeared disinterested in the whole conversation. Her mind was elsewhere, and Tess knew where.

"Tell us your good news, Letitia," Marlene said quickly before Rex, who was staring bullets at Justin, decided to react to Justin's chuckle.

"Before I came downstairs, I phoned home for my messages. There was one from the Hennessey Fabric Corporation. They're interested in sponsoring me in a quilting program on TV."

"Hennessey?" Marlene said. "They're the people who sponsor Cassie's show."

Letitia nodded eagerly. "Naturally, with Cassie . . . er, gone, they're looking for a replacement. They still have four of her programs on tape, and they'll run them before they start a new series. That doesn't give them much time to find somebody."

Marlene was looking skeptical. "Why did they contact *you*?" Her tone was faintly challenging, as though she doubted the Hennessey Corporation would chose Letitia from among the best quilters in the country, a couple of whom were seated at the Iris House breakfast table.

Letitia put her hands out, palms up, and shrugged. If she was offended by Marlene's skepticism, she hid it well.

"Maybe it's because I approached them a year or so ago about doing a program. At that time, of course, Cassie's program was getting good ratings, so they returned the videotape I sent and said they'd keep my letter on file. Now it seems they want to see the tape again. I'm so excited, I—"

"Wait a minute," Rex interrupted. "Cassie died on Wednesday and today is Friday. How did they find out so soon?"

Letitia hesitated. A rosy blush crept up her neck. "Well—I sent them a fax Wednesday night from a copy shop."

"My goodness, aren't you helpful," commented Phyllis with a lifted eyebrow.

Letitia's blush deepened. "That was certainly my intention. I knew they'd need some time to find a replacement."

Now Rex's face was flushed, too, but not with embarrassment. "Namely you," he snapped angrily. "Good God, Letitia, the woman's body is hardly cold yet."

A sarcastic sneer settled around Justin's mouth. "Oops. Letitia beat you to it, didn't she, Rex?"

"I resent that!" Rex retorted. "I simply can't believe Letitia would do something so crass and tasteless."

An angry spark lit Letitia's eyes. So she *can* lose her temper, Tess thought, watching this new side of Letitia with interest. Rex's description of her as crass and tasteless didn't sit at all well.

"Get off your high horse, Rex," Phyllis put in. "You don't care a fig about how it looks. You couldn't stand the sight of Cassie."

"That's beside the point!"

"Come on, Rex old man," Justin said laconically. "Letitia saw her chance and grabbed it. It's exactly what Cassie would have done."

Letitia looked flustered. "Of course she would have.

Why—'' She stopped abruptly as her eyes fell on Marlene. The others followed her gaze and had the grace to look embarrassed. They'd evidently forgotten that one of Cassie's closest friends was sitting there while they insulted the dead woman.

"That's enough." Marlene bristled. "I won't sit here and let you malign Cassie. Honestly, you people are a bunch of vultures." She wadded her napkin in one hand, dropped it on the table, pushed back her chair, and stood.

"Marlene," Tess said quickly, "may I speak to you in private?" She'd decided that it would be easier to talk to Mary if she took Mary's old friend Marlene with her.

"All right," Marlene said, if a bit hesitantly.

"I'll come up to your room in a couple of minutes."

Marlene strode from the dining room. They heard her footsteps receding up the stairs.

Shannon rose from her chair. "She's absolutely right. Greedy carrion, the lot of you." With that flat announcement, she followed Marlene up the stairs.

Expressions on the remaining faces in the dining room ranged from amusement to surprise. It was the first thing Shannon had said since Tess had joined her guests. Perhaps they'd forgotten her presence.

Letitia finally broke the silence. "I didn't see anything wrong with notifying Cassie's sponsors," she said, fumbling with her napkin. After placing it beside her plate, she stood. "I'm sorry if I've offended anybody." She left the table.

"Devious old witch," Rex mumbled.

"A bit like the pot and the kettle, Rex," Justin mumbled into his coffee cup.

Miranda woke suddenly, with no sense of what time it was. She switched on the light and went to the bedroom window, pulling the drapes aside.

A hazy blue sky. Grass still sparkling with diamonds of dew. Maxwell curled up on the wicker chaise. She tapped on the glass. Maxwell lifted his head, looked around, but didn't see her. Suddenly she felt exposed, as though she were being watched. Until Cassie Terhune's murder, she'd had a sense of being safe and protected in Victoria Springs. Now she didn't feel completely safe anywhere. She really hoped she'd get back to feeling normal again soon. She let the drape fall back into place and remembered what had awakened her. The telephone. It had rung twice before her mother had answered in another part of the house.

It was seven forty-five, too late to go back to bed, and she didn't think she could sleep, anyway, because she was so worried about her mother. She laid out fresh jeans and a plaid cotton shirt, then went into her bathroom to shower.

Fifteen minutes later, she found her mother at the kitchen table with a cup of coffee. "Hi."

Mary turned her head and made the effort to smile. "Good morning, honey."

"Did you sleep OK?"

"Like a log. Only now I feel sluggish." She raked a limp lock of hair from her eyes. "Those pills always do that to me. I really hate taking them."

"I'm glad you did this time."

"Want me to make oatmeal?"

Miranda shook her head. She went to the pantry and took down a box of cornflakes. "I'll eat cold cereal." She found a bowl. "Who was that on the phone?"

"When? Oh—yes. Wrong number." Mary looked away almost furtively. Miranda suspected she was lying about the phone call. Maybe it had been Shannon again, and Mary didn't want to worry her.

"Are you going to the quilt show today?"

"A little later. But you need to be there when it opens. I asked Kendra's mother to come by for you."

"When?"

"Eight-thirty."

"No, I mean, like when did you ask her."

"I phoned her a few minutes ago."

After that "wrong number"? There was no need for Mrs. Lawson to come by for her. Kendra could handle the home ec booth for an hour, until Miranda and Mary got there. Obviously her mother didn't want her around.

"Oh, I almost forgot. Tess Darcy called last night. She said to tell you she'd be by here at eight-thirty. She wants to talk to you before you go to the quilt show."

Mary frowned. "What about?"

"She didn't say." Miranda had wondered herself why Tess was coming there. What was so important that Tess was making a special trip to the house? Couldn't she talk to Mary on the phone?

Mary was gazing out the window now. She didn't seem to know or care what Tess wanted. But even if she'd known, she wouldn't have told Miranda. Nobody told her anything.

Consumed with curiosity, Miranda added sugar and milk to her cereal. Thinking her own thoughts, she stood at the kitchen counter to eat.

She hoped that it wouldn't be something terrible, whatever Tess wanted to talk to her mother about. Ever since the quilt show started, awful things had been happening to her mother. First, those boards fell off the loft and almost killed her. Then Cassie Terhune was murdered in the quilt guild's booth. It had made Miranda ask herself questions she was afraid to examine too closely. Like was somebody trying to hurt her mother? Had the murderer known it was Cassie Terhune he attacked in the dark, instead of Mary? To top things off, Shannon Diamond was going around asking her own nosy questions about Miranda's parents. What was *that* all about?

Miranda had started out liking Shannon. But when they'd had lunch at the Sampler Tea Room, she'd realized that there was something too intense about her. She never seemed to relax. It wore you out.

Miranda sighed. She wouldn't be accepting any more lunch invitations from Shannon Diamond, should more be offered, which she doubted. Shannon had gotten all the information she could from Miranda, so why waste money on more lunches?

She glanced at her watch, hoping that Mrs. Lawson didn't arrive before Tess Darcy. She didn't like the idea of leaving her mother in the house alone again. Cool it, she told herself. If it came to that, it would be for only a few minutes.

At least her mother seemed rested and not so nervous this morning, as she'd been yesterday when Miranda had come down to breakfast to find her pacing restlessly through the house, which she had been doing for hours. Miranda knew this because every time she woke up in the night, she'd heard her mother moving around. She'd gotten up once to see if Mary was sick, but Mary had said no, she just couldn't sleep. At that point, Miranda realized her mother couldn't get the horrible sight of Cassie Terhune and all that blood out of her mind.

When Miranda came into the kitchen yesterday morning, the coffeemaker had been almost empty, so Miranda assumed her mother had already drunk several cups, which must have contributed to her tense state. She had known better than to comment on it, though. But then she'd made the mistake of arguing with Mary about whether she should go to the quilt show or stay with Mary, and her mother had gotten so worked up that she'd yelled at Miranda and thrown a photograph on the floor and broken the glass.

Her mother's reaction had very nearly thrown Miranda into shock. Mary hardly ever lost her temper and yelled.

Until recently, in fact, Miranda had worried that her mother was too quiet and withdrawn most of the time. She knew why, of course; it was because of what her father had done. Her mother had never used the word "suicide" in Miranda's presence, but she knew her father had killed himself. It wasn't easy for Miranda, either, but it had happened. She missed her dad all the time, but it didn't change anything to mope around in a depression.

Actually, Miranda assured herself, it was probably good for her mother to get mad and yell and throw things. Maybe it would help her get over her grief. Keeping her sadness to herself sure hadn't helped.

Outside, a car horn blared.

"There's your ride," Mary said.

Miranda scooped up a final bite of cereal and milk, grabbed a napkin to wipe her mouth, and set the bowl in the sink. She hesitated. "Well, I guess I'll go."

"Better hurry."

"Bye."

Looking over her shoulder, Mary made a shooing motion with one hand. "See you in a little while."

After leaving the breakfast table, Tess had gone to the Annabel Jane Room and asked Marlene to accompany her to Mary's house, explaining only that she was worried about Mary. Marlene had agreed to go, then told Tess a little more about her conversation with Ralph Terhune. Ralph had expressed surprise that the police had questioned him so thoroughly. Evidently he was a suspect, but he'd eventually been able to satisfy them that he had been in Kansas City when Cassie was killed.

Noticing that Marlene looked even more washed out than she had at breakfast, against the lacy whites and ruffled lavenders of her room, Tess asked cautiously, "What else did Ralph Terhune tell them?"

"He didn't say specifically."

Tess let it drop. She had meant to broach the real reason for the visit on the drive from Iris House, but as they left Marlene had said she'd take her own car and go straight to the quilt show from Mary's.

At Mary's, Marlene pulled into the driveway behind Tess. They got out and went up to the front door. A couple of blue jays were quarreling in a maple tree, and a whippoorwill mocked them. Even with that haze in the sky, it was going to be another beautiful day. Tess hoped she could find time for a walk later.

As Mary opened the door, Tess heard another car squeal to a stop at the curb out front. Twisting around, she saw Shannon Diamond scramble out of her car and hurry across the front lawn.

Ignoring Shannon, Mary glanced from Tess to Marlene. "I didn't know you were coming, too, Marlene."

"I'm here at Tess's invitation," Marlene told her.

Mary fixed curious eyes on Tess.

"Never mind Marlene," Tess said. "What's Shannon doing here?"

By that time Shannon was close enough to hear Tess's words. "Not that it's any of your business, Tess, but I have an appointment!" She folded her arms across her chest and stared Tess down.

Glancing uneasily at Tess, Mary confirmed Shannon's words. "Shannon called this morning and asked if she could come by. I saw no reason to say no."

Marlene darted a quizzical look at Tess. Obviously she was wondering what was going on with the other three.

So much for giving Mary a private warning of Shannon's intentions. Tess groaned inwardly as she followed Mary into the house. This was taking on the aspects of a scene from Greek tragedy.

"Would anybody like coffee?" Mary asked, hovering in

the doorway to the den. She looked pale and puffy-eyed, possibly the result of her drugged sleep the previous night. Shannon had marched straight to an armchair and sat stiffly on the edge of the seat, her hands gripping her purse as if to keep herself from going into orbit. Tess and Marlene sat on either end of the sofa.

"Nothing for me," Tess said.

"Me, either," Marlene added.

Shannon ignored the question and went on the attack. "I thought this was going to be a private conversation."

Mary pulled out a footstool and sat down next to the sofa with a world-weary look. "I can't imagine what you could have to say that Tess and Marlene can't hear."

"Oh, *really*?" One corner of Shannon's mouth curled up. "Well, if you don't mind, why should I?"

"Shannon!" Tess put in. "Let me talk to Mary first."

Shannon thrust out her chin. "No way. I'm not leaving until we've had this out."

"What's going on here?" Marlene asked sharply. She looked at Mary in total bewilderment.

Mary shook her head. "I have no idea."

She honestly doesn't, Tess thought, and felt her stomach muscles tighten in sympathy with Mary.

With an angry jerk, Shannon unzipped her purse and pulled out the birth certificate Tess had seen in her room at Iris House. "This will clear it up for you," she bit out and threw it in Mary's direction. It fluttered in the air before landing near Mary's feet.

Plainly confused, Mary picked up the birth certificate, unfolded it, and read it. When she looked up, her face was a study in amazement. "Whose birth certificate is this?"

Shannon stared at her. "The baby you gave away. Me."

Tess heard Marlene stifle a small gasp, but she was watching Mary, whose mouth hung open. The first sound that came out was a shrill laugh, which told Tess that Mary was still a bundle of nerves. Finally, Mary gathered herself together and said, "You can't be serious."

"Oh, right." Shannon's laugh verged on hysteria. "I'm making it all up."

Mary peered at her closely. "Are you?"

"Why would I do that?"

Mary shook her head unhappily. "I can't imagine. Obviously you believe what you're saying, but you've made a terrible mistake, Shannon."

"Are you trying to say your maiden name wasn't Mary Lane?"

"Oh, that was my name"—she waved the certificate in the air—"but it evidently hasn't occurred to you that it's a pretty common name. I'm not the Mary Lane named here."

Tess glanced at Marlene, who was sitting forward on the sofa, intently following the interchange between Mary and Shannon. She looked dazed and totally at sea and as if she wished she were anywhere else but where she was. Tess felt guilty. She was having second thoughts about bringing Marlene into this.

As for Shannon, she was taken aback by Mary's flat denial. She must have expected anything but that. Tears, excuses, pleas, but not denial. "Look at the birthplace," Shannon said. "That's just a few miles from Kansas City. I know you were living in Kansas City then. You told me so yourself."

"That's true, but—"

Shannon suddenly jumped up. "Stop it! Stop lying." She was shaking, and her voice had a desperate edge. "Twenty-five years ago last July twenty-sixth, you gave birth to a baby girl and put her up for adoption."

Mary remained admirably calm. "No," she said gently. "It wasn't me, Shannon." She refolded the certificate and stood, taking a tentative step toward Shannon, as if to touch her.

Shannon flinched away. "You don't need to worry. I don't want to be a part of your life if you don't want me. I just want some answers. Who was my father? Why did you give me away?"

"I'm not your mother, Shannon," Mary said dully. "I'm sorry."

Shannon's eyes filled with tears. "But it says . . ."

Marlene stirred, got to her feet. She was utterly shaken. "I'm not needed here. We'll talk later, Mary. No, you needn't see me out."

She lifted a hand and placed it on the back of a chair to steady herself, then left the room quickly without looking at anyone.

Tess's gaze followed Marlene. Oddly, she seemed more upset than Mary. "I shouldn't have included her in this," Tess said. "I'm sorry, Mary. I just thought, since she's an old friend of yours, that it would be a comfort to have her here. I wanted to warn you before you spoke to Shannon."

"You already knew why Shannon was asking all those questions, why she insisted on coming here today?"

"I only found out yesterday afternoon," Tess said. "I asked Shannon not to disturb you until you'd had some rest."

"You think I'm Shannon's mother, too, don't you?"

"I did," Tess admitted, "but if you say you aren't, that's good enough for me."

Mary sank back down on the footstool. "Twenty-five years ago last July," she said musingly. "That was the summer I met Gerald. At a friend's wedding in June. Another friend introduced us. I was working as a secretary and he was getting a master's degree in finance at the university in Lawrence." She smiled sadly. "We spent all our spare time together. I remember my friends complaining that they never saw me anymore. We were engaged the following summer but we didn't marry until Gerald finished school and had a job." She looked up at Shannon, misty-eyed. "Believe me, Shannon, I was not having a baby that summer. In one way this is ironic, given that we tried for several years after we were married and had almost given up when I found out I was pregnant with Miranda."

After a long moment, Shannon wiped her eyes, with the back of her hand. She looked forlorn and utterly defeated, and very young. "I guess I'll have to believe you."

"If I were your mother, I wouldn't deny it. In fact, I'd be very proud."

Shannon looked at her narrowly. "You really mean that?"

"Of course I do. A smart, pretty, successful young woman like you would make any mother proud."

After a pause, Shannon nodded. "Thank you. It's just— I've searched for my mother for so long and I thought I'd found her."

"I understand," Mary said. She handed the birth certificate back to Shannon.

Shannon thrust it into her purse, pulled out a tissue, wiped her eyes, and blew her nose. "My Lord," she said tearily, "yesterday at the quilt show, when I found out you'd stayed home, I almost told Miranda I was her sister." She stuffed the used tissue back in her purse. "Thank heaven I didn't."

"Yes," said Mary fervently.

"I—I'd better go," Shannon said. Her gaze flitted from Mary to Tess and back to Mary. "I guess I made a nuisance of myself. I'm sorry I bothered you."

"It was not a bother, exactly," Mary said. "It was just puzzling. I only wish we could have cleared this up sooner."

Neither Mary nor Tess spoke as Shannon left the house.

The sound of her car starting out front seemed to release them from a spell.

"Well . . ." said Tess.

"At least I know why she was asking all those questions about me and Gerald. I'm sorry for her. It must be terrible, not knowing who your parents are."

Tess murmured an assent.

"Thanks for trying to help, Tess."

"A lot of help I was," said Tess ruefully.

"You tried. Now I really need to get ready to go to the quilt show."

"Go ahead. I'll let myself out."

Mary left the room and Tess heard her on the uncarpeted stairs. She turned to leave, then reversed herself and went to the lamp table near the window. She wanted another look at the photograph she'd seen yesterday. She pulled open the drawer in the table and carefully lifted out the picture with the broken glass. She studied the six smiling faces. The Terhunes—Cassie looked very much as she had looked when she died. She hadn't aged as noticeably as the other women.

Mary had been thinner then, her brown hair worn in a youthful, shoulder-length style. On the other hand, Marlene had probably weighed ten pounds more than she did today. Her face looked fuller. Or was that an illusion, created by her teased hair-do?

Staring at the picture, Tess was again struck by a feeling of having seen the picture, or somebody in it, in another context. She bent to peer more closely at the faces.

Cassie's smile was somehow triumphant. Strange, she hadn't noticed that before. Mary looked happy. Marlene's half-smile looked almost secretive, as though she were hiding something.

Suddenly, Tess knew what had been nagging at her.

Shannon's lips had formed that same half-smile a few minutes ago.

Tess's first instinct was to deny what she was thinking. Shannon and Marlene had barely spoken to each other. Once or twice, Tess had even gotten the impression that Shannon didn't like Marlene very much.

Her second thought was, Dear Lord, what a tangled web.

Should she call Mary back, ask her opinion? No, that wouldn't be right. And who else could she discuss it with? Perhaps it was better to let sleeping dogs lie.

She replaced the picture in the drawer and closed it. Quietly, she left the house.

Chapter 15

The exhibition hall was crowded by the time Tess got there, and it was only Friday. Saturday and Sunday would be mob scenes.

Rose Cline was taking care of the Drunkard's Path booth until Mary arrived. Tess waved to her as she passed and stopped long enough at the home ec booth to tell Miranda that her mother was on the way.

Marlene's booth was unattended. Tess passed it and stopped at the Hydes' booth. "Have you seen Marlene?"

"She was in her booth a few minutes ago," Justin said.

"I saw her heading in the direction of the ladies' room," Phyllis put in.

Which would have been the next place Tess looked. Marlene would need some time to compose herself. Tess crossed to the main aisle and walked back to the rest room.

Marlene was seated on the couch, her head in her hands. She didn't move when Tess entered. Tess bent to look beneath the cubicles, making sure they were alone.

"Marlene?"

She looked up. Her eyes were blurred by tears.

"Is there anything I can do for you?"

She straightened, clasped her hands in her lap, and shook her head. When a long moment passed and she didn't speak, Tess realized she was still trying to collect herself after what must have been the biggest shock of her life. Tess sat down beside Marlene and patted her clasped hands.

Marlene swallowed two or three times and eventually managed to say brokenly, "You know, don't you?"

"I guessed."

"How did I give myself away?"

"It wasn't that. It was a picture I saw at Mary's house, a picture of the six of you—the Terhunes, the Frankses, and you and your husband . . ."

"I know the one you mean." Marlene sucked in oxygen, let it out slowly. Her voice steadied. "It was taken eleven or twelve years ago. The six of us went on a Carribean cruise. That was Cassie's idea—to celebrate her big promotion at the Hexler Corporation."

"I noticed the picture yesterday, but I didn't realize until I saw it again today that Shannon looks like you, at least like you did then—something about the mouth and chin. And sometimes she sort of half-smiles, the way you do."

Marlene sank back on the couch. "Do you really think she looks like me?" Her expression hovered between hope and fear.

"I doubt that anybody else will have noticed the similarities."

She chewed her bottom lip, clasped and unclasped her hands reflexively. "*I* didn't even notice. I had no idea why Shannon was there this morning until she pulled out that birth certificate and threw it at Mary."

Just as Tess had feared. No wonder Marlene had looked dismayed and had to balance herself against the chair as she left.

"We never had children, Mike and I," Marlene murmured as if to herself. "We wanted them, but it never happened."

Tess was not surprised to learn that Mike was not Shannon's father. "I'm sorry," was all she could think of to say. It didn't seem like nearly enough.

"I've always wondered if my barrenness—after Shannon—was some kind of punishment."

The woman must have spent twenty-five years burdened by guilt because she gave away her baby. "You know that's absurd," Tess said.

When she looked at Tess, her eyes were red, filled with pain, like open wounds. "Is it? I broke one of God's commandments: Thou shall not commit adultery."

Adultery? The word gave Tess pause. She had been imagining Marlene young and single and desperate. "You and Mike were already married when Shannon was born?"

She nodded dumbly.

Tess could literally feel the agony emanating from Marlene in waves, agony she had been carrying for twenty-five years. Had Mike insisted that she give the baby up because it wasn't his? Had she agreed because he'd made her choose between him and the child?

"We married a few weeks before he went to Vietnam. I thought I couldn't bear the loneliness. I—I started going to bars in the evenings. Then one night I drank too much. There was a man—his name was Richard. I—I never even knew his last name."

Father's name, unknown

She clutched Tess's hand. "It only happened once," she said, as if it was vital that Tess believe her.

"Oh, Marlene . . ."

"I know it's the same trite, sordid story many women could tell. Only it doesn't seem trite when it happens to you."

"Of course not," Tess murmured, wishing she knew

something comforting to say. But Marlene had gone beyond the comfort of mere words years ago.

"When I realized I was pregnant, abortion was . . . well, it was out of the question as far as I was concerned. I couldn't tell Mike. He was so young—we both were. I could never have made him understand. So—" She turned her hands over, stared at the palms.

"He might have surprised you, if you'd told him."

She swallowed. "I should have. I knew that afterward, when it was much too late to change anything."

"Why didn't you go to your parents . . . friends?"

"It seems silly now, but I was too ashamed. My parents were in Washington state. After the fifth month, when I couldn't hide my condition any longer, I didn't visit them. My friends were . . . well, I didn't feel I could confide in them, either. Most of them were single, dating, interested in having fun. I felt different, totally cut off from them. I was so depressed that I hardly left the house. Friends tried to make a date for lunch or coffee a few times, and then they gave up. After my marriage, I hadn't seen them as often, anyway. The last two months, I rented a room in a little town outside Kansas City and saw a doctor at the clinic there."

"Under a false name?"

She nodded, pressed her fingers to her eyelids, squeezing out tears. Tess found a tissue in her purse and handed it over. Marlene blotted her cheeks.

"Once, years afterward, I almost confided in Cassie. I didn't know her when—when it happened. Later—five or six years later—Cassie and I were both trying to get pregnant, and I almost let the whole story slip out. But I covered up and I don't think Cassie suspected what I'd started to tell her."

Thinking of how shrewd Cassie had been, Tess wondered about that.

"Strange as it seems, the hardest part would have been telling Cassie that I'd used Mary's name."

"Why did you do it, Marlene?"

"I didn't plan it. When I first visited the doctor, I meant to give a common name that would be difficult to trace. I had decided to use Mary Smith and to say that I was unmarried. Then—I don't know what happened—but when the nurse asked my name, 'Mary Lane' just popped out. I heard myself and couldn't believe what I'd said. It was unconscious, I suppose, because I was a nervous wreck and that was the name of one of my best friends. Then I didn't see how I could take it back. How I could explain . . ."

Tess understood how it could have happened, when Marlene was so young and scared. "So that's the name they put on the birth certificate," she said. She could imagine Marlene then, at twenty or twenty-one. Her young husband in a foreign land fighting a war that few understood, pregnant with another man's child, terrified that someone would find out. She understood why Marlene would have been incapable of informing her husband via airmail. It would have seemed so cruel, like forcing Mike to pay for her mistake.

"The doctor arranged for a private adoption. He said they'd issue a new birth certificate with the adoptive parents' names on it."

"They probably did. But evidently they kept the original record somewhere—for all I know the law requires it. Anyway, Shannon found it with the help of a search group. Marlene—" Tess halted as two women came into the rest room, talking. They fell silent when they saw Marlene and Tess and exchanged questioning glances as they entered two cubicles. Nobody said another word until the women had left.

Then it was Marlene who spoke. "I've wondered for

years what I'd do if this ever happened and I still don't know."

Tess said, "There's something my mother used to tell me. I was grown before I learned that Robert Frost said it first. 'The best way out is always through.'"

Marlene nodded gloomily. "You mean I should talk to Shannon and tell Mike."

Tess nodded.

"And then I'd have to tell Mary that I'd used her name."

"Yes."

Marlene pushed out a gulp of air. "Let the chips fall. In one way, it would be a huge relief, no matter what happened next. Sort of like getting a heavy pack off my back. But Mike—"

"You're not giving your husband much credit," Tess said.

She almost smiled. "I guess I'm not."

"You've been together more than twenty-five years. Don't you think he'd understand?"

She thought about it. "Maybe. Probably, once he got over the hurt. But I can't just go out there and—" She shook her head. "No, I have to think about it, Tess. I don't want to make another terrible mistake. You won't—?"

"It's not my secret to tell," Tess said.

Marlene got up and turned on the faucet over the washbasin. She splashed cold water on her face and held a paper towel over her eyes for several moments. Then she wadded it and tossed it into the waste container. "I need to be by myself," she said. "I think I'll go outside and walk around the grounds. Could you possibly tend my booth for a while, Tess?"

"Of course."

Troubled, Tess watched Marlene straighten her spine, lift her head, and leave the rest room.

Chapter 16

It was after eight o'clock, and the stars were hidden by the hazy cloud cover that had blurred the sky all day. Street lamps, however, provided enough illumination for a walk through the streets of Victoria Springs, which Tess had been determined to have before she retired. She and Luke had walked from Iris House to Harry's Grill, a block north of Cinny's Queen Street Book Shop, for burgers and fries. At the moment, they were strolling back toward Iris House on Maple Avenue, hands clasped between them.

After walking a full block in silence, Luke asked, "When are you going to tell me what's bearing so heavily on your mind?"

Tess started involuntarily as his words jerked her attention back to him. "I'm just tired," she said, grateful for the nighttime shadows. Luke knew her too well. If he could have seen her effort to erase the troubled frown from her face, he'd have known she was evading his question.

But her tone must have given her away. He halted beneath a street lamp and peered into her face. "*Au contraire*, my love. Your mind is deep in something heavy."

185

"OK, I admit it." They walked on. "I'm worried about the police investigation. Except for Rex Brindle, Butts has talked to no one since Thursday morning. That could mean he's reached a dead end."

"Not necessarily. Maybe he's come up with additional suspects—people who don't happen to be staying at Iris House."

Tess thought of what Marlene had told her, that Butts had questioned Ralph Terhune thoroughly. If only there was a way to find out what Terhune had said. "If so," she said, "he's sure playing his cards close to his chest."

Luke chuckled. "You were assuming Butts would have informed you if he had other suspects?"

"Hardly! But the murderer has to be somebody in town for the quilt show, somebody who killed Cassie by mistake. We've already decided that."

She could see well enough to catch his cocked eyebrow. "*You* decided, as I recall."

"And you agreed."

He squeezed her hand. "I don't remember, but even if I did, I'm having second thoughts. If the intended victim was Mary Franks, why hasn't the killer tried again?"

It was not a new question to Tess; she'd been asking it of herself all day. Now she verbalized the same possibilities she'd previously voiced only in her thoughts. "Maybe he's decided to wait, let things cool off before he makes another attempt. Besides, Mary has been warned. She's on guard now."

"On the other hand, there may have been no mistake. If the killer was after Cassie, he's done what he set out to do, and there will be no further attempts."

Tess started to protest, then held back as she thought about Luke's words.

And Nedra's. *Turn things around. Look at things different*, had been Nedra's advice. It was worth more consideration. So, suppose Cassie *was* the intended victim after all. Even suppose Ralph Terhune's alibi wasn't as tight as the police evidently believed. But, no, he couldn't have been at the quilt show without *somebody* seeing him.

"The problem is," Luke went on, "we're operating from a base of ignorance."

"What do you mean?"

"There's too much we don't know about Cassie and Mary and the others. There could be past wrongs, old grudges, intertwined relationships that we know nothing about."

Tangled webs, Tess thought. Such as the fact that Marlene Oxley had given birth to a baby girl twenty-five years ago and had given it up for adoption, without anyone knowing, not even her husband. The fact that the child was Shannon Diamond, who had tracked her mother as far as Victoria Springs. How ironic that Marlene's and Shannon's presence in Victoria Springs had coincided with the murder. But she couldn't say any of this to Luke. She'd given Marlene her word.

It didn't stop her wondering what Shannon would do, now that she knew Mary Franks wasn't her birth mother. Would she give up the search? Tess didn't think so. Shannon was very determined. And angry at her birth mother for giving her away. Tess didn't think Shannon would be able to put her questions to rest until she had some answers.

And what did any of that have to do with Cassie's murder? At one point, Tess had even entertained the thought that Shannon had killed the wrong person in a frustrated rage. Upon reflection, she reminded herself that Shannon was after answers to where she came from. She couldn't get answers if she killed the woman she believed to be her mother.

Furthermore, if Cassie was the intended victim all along, Shannon seemed an even less likely murderer. She claimed she had never met Cassie before her arrival at Iris House. It must be true, or Cassie would have mentioned having known Shannon before.

Either way, Shannon had now slipped off Tess's suspect list. She had no motive. The fact that her search had placed her in Victoria Springs at the time of the murder now appeared to be pure coincidence.

With Shannon off the suspect list, who was left? The Hydes, Marlene Oxley, Rex Brindle, Letitia Lattimore. None of them seemed to have a bone to pick with Mary.

Which brought Tess back to Cassie as the intended victim. Maybe she had been looking in the wrong place all along. Certainly Cassie, unlike Mary, had enemies. Even her ex-husband had said that she used people. Letitia had wanted to take over Cassie's TV show and Rex had accused her of stealing his designs. Even though Tess supposed murders had been committed for reasons as improbable as those, she just couldn't envision Letitia or Rex carrying out a premeditated murder on such grounds.

"You're doing it again."

Luke's voice tore her from the morass of her thoughts. "I'm sorry, and I'm getting nowhere. I think you're right, Luke. There are connections we haven't made, too much we simply don't know."

"Then please stop thinking about it."

"I'll try." Easy to say, Tess thought, but not so easy to stop the silent questions spinning in her brain.

"I'm beginning to feel neglected," Luke said in an offended tone that was uncharacteristic of him. "All you think about lately is the murder."

"I'm sorry, sweetheart. But I think of you more than you know."

He stopped and wrapped his arms around her. "Tell me more."

* * *

Saturday afternoon, Tess finally found time to browse all the booths at the quilt show. A great deal of the merchandise had been purchased and carried away, but some fine items remained.

Tess, who still wanted to purchase a decorative piece for Iris House, spent twenty minutes examining every remaining quilt in Rex Brindle's booth. If possible, Rex was in a worse mood than yesterday. His mouth arranged in a sullen pout, he watched her broodingly as she looked and touched and turned pieces over to examine the stitching on the back. It was fine needlework, no doubt about that. But the prices!

"I'm sorry, I can't read this one," Tess said, pointing to the price tag on a black and mauve wall hanging. "Is that eleven hundred?"

Rex stood in a corner of the booth, his arms folded across his chest. "Correct. And I don't discount my work, so you needn't bother haggling."

What an ego the man had! "I wasn't about to," Tess retorted. She moved on to another piece.

"You get what you pay for," Rex observed darkly.

"I'm sure you're right," Tess said, "but I don't have an unlimited budget. I'll just have to find a nice piece that's within my price range."

Rex made a huffing sound, as though to say her budget was no concern of his. "If price is your main concern, you'd have better luck at some of the cheaper booths." He emphasized the adjective as though it were a dirty word.

Tess eyed him with interest, wondering how he ever made a sale if he was this churlish with all his customers. Rex obviously couldn't wait to close up shop and leave Victoria Springs. "May I ask you a question, Rex?"

He spread his legs and rocked back on his heels. "You can *ask*."

"Why are you so angry?"

A vein throbbed in his neck. "You'd be, too, if you were being accused of murder."

"Who's accusing you?"

"Besides the police, you mean?" he inquired sarcastically. "Well, let's see. For starters, everybody at Iris House thinks I did it, including you."

"I never said—"

He overrode her reasoned defense. "You don't have to say it. The way you all acted at breakfast the last two days, I might as well be carrying typhoid."

The atmosphere had been noticeably subdued at the breakfast table, but Tess thought Rex was reading far too much into his table companions' behavior. Which could be contributed to a guilty conscience. She was trying to take Nedra's and Luke's advice today and pursue her private investigation with a more open mind. She was, for one thing, still mulling the possibility that Cassie Terhune had been the murderer's target from the beginning.

"I think you're overstating the case, Rex."

"But people aren't trying to frame you for murder, are they?"

"Oh, really—"

"Let me tell you something," he interrupted, flushing. "Cassie Terhune was hell on wheels. Had she lived, I would have destroyed her reputation in court. Frankly, I'm sorry I won't have the opportunity now. I refuse to alter my assessment of her character because she's dead."

"As far as I know, nobody has suggested you change your opinion." Besides having a bloated ego, the man was the classic bullheaded personality described in clichés. Cutting off one's nose to spite one's face came to Tess's mind. "You might be a little more judicious in voicing it, however." Come to think of it, Cassie had given him similar advice during that argument Tess had overheard in the Iris House foyer. In fact, she had threatened to charge him with slander if he continued to call her a thief. As a lawyer, Cassie knew how to use the legal system to her own advantage. Had Rex realized that? It was possible he wasn't as sure about his chances in court as he claimed. It was also possible that he'd decided to mete out his own justice.

An elderly woman with a cane came up to the booth and began talking to Rex, who actually seemed to make an effort to be pleasant. Tess took the opportunity to slip away. Rex's prices were too rich for her blood, and his work too contemporary. A traditional piece would be more in keeping with Iris House's Victorian style and furnishings.

Intending to give Letitia's traditional pieces a closer look, Tess caught sight of Marlene Oxley in her booth and took a detour. Marlene looked more rested today, though her demeanor gave away her sober state of mind. Two lines seemed to have permanently etched themselves between her eyebrows, and her mouth turned down at the corners. At breakfast, however, she had done an admirable job of seeming to pay no more attention to Shannon than to the other guests. Tess was certain no one else had noticed how Marlene's quick, furtive glances drank in her daughter whenever Shannon's attention was elsewhere.

Marlene was making a sale when Tess stopped at the booth. She made change, handed the customer her purchase, and waited for the woman to leave. Turning to Tess, she said, "I talked to Mike this morning."

"About Shannon?"

One corner of Marlene's mouth turned up in a faint smile. "I lost my nerve. Anyway, I decided I can't tell him something like that on the telephone."

"But you *are* going to tell him?" Tess looked at Marlene with concern.

Marlene seemed to stand straighter before she replied. "It's something I have to do, Tess. I think I knew that before I left Mary's house yesterday. I just had to come to terms with it.''

However Marlene's husband reacted, Tess thought, the mere unburdening of the twenty-five-year-old secret would be like a fresh breeze blowing through the murky corners of Marlene's mind. In less than forty-eight hours, she would be with her husband. The quilt show closed Sunday afternoon. Marlene planned to leave Victoria Springs then and drive straight through to Kansas City.

"Will you tell Shannon before you leave Victoria Springs?" Tess asked.

"I haven't decided that yet, but I can't put off telling Mary that I used her name. I hope it doesn't destroy our friendship.'' She looked pained. "I've already lost one friend this week.'' She turned to the man who had approached the booth. "Hello. May I help you with something?''

As the man began to explain that he wanted to buy a quilt for his wife's birthday, Tess caught Marlene's eye, waved, and left the booth. She thought that Marlene had made the right decision. It was clear to Tess that Marlene hungered for the daughter she'd never known. Tess was not even sure that Marlene had been consciously aware of the hunger until she'd been forced to acknowledge the identity of her daughter in Mary Franks's den. Before that, Tess supposed Marlene had spent twenty-five years trying to assuage her guilt feelings by telling herself the child she gave away was better off. It had taken Shannon's relentless determination to find her mother to shake Marlene into the realization that she had never forgiven herself.

It was sad that Marlene hadn't unburdened herself years ago, but Tess could understand how terrifying the mere thought of doing it must have been. Yet she had once been on the verge of confiding in Cassie Terhune.

Tess frowned a little as she remembered Marlene's

words. . . . *but I covered up and I don't think Cassie suspected* . . . How likely was it that the clever Cassie had never, during all those years, suspected? What would Cassie have done if she *had* suspected? Even from her brief, casual acquaintanceship with Cassie, Tess knew she hadn't been one to skirt issues or mince words.

If Cassie had discovered Marlene's secret and confronted her with it, Marlene's first reaction would have been to deny it vehemently and demand that Cassie stop talking about it. But what if Cassie wouldn't stop? What if she'd threatened to force the issue, tell Marlene's husband—all in Marlene's best interests, of course?

What if Marlene had decided to shut her up for good?

Tess didn't like the direction her thoughts were taking. She was grateful for the distraction of looking through Letitia's handiwork.

"This one would be perfect for your guest parlor," Letitia said, unfolding a quilt made up of six-inch blocks in shades of gray, rose, and pink separated by three-inch forest green sashes. The edges were finished with a deep rose figured border and a forest-green binding.

"What is this pattern?" Tess asked, running her hand over the close, meticulous quilting.

"Card Tricks."

Letitia was right. The colors were ideal for the guest parlor. "It's lovely." Trying not to be too obvious, Tess turned over the tag attached to the quilt and read the price.

Letitia looked a little anxious. "For you, I'll knock off fifty dollars."

It was still a lot of money, but only half the cost of one of Rex Brindle's wall hangings. "Sold," Tess decided. "It's so beautiful, how can I refuse?"

Letitia smiled and took the quilt from Tess to refold it. "I'm so glad you aren't mad at me, too," she said as she bent to retrieve a large sack from beneath the counter.

Tess wasn't sure she'd heard correctly. "Mad at you? Why would I be mad at you?"

Flushing, Letitia stuffed the quilt into the sack. "Because I faxed the news of Cassie's death to her sponsors. Everybody else acts like I did something horrible. You'd think I'd kil—" She halted mid-word, flushing a bright red.

You'd think I'd killed her. That's what she'd started to say before she thought better of it. Tess's suspicions kicked into high gear. Letitia wanted that TV show, and she'd known she'd never get it with Cassie in the picture. But was that a motive for murder?

Tess felt guilty standing before the woman with such thoughts. To hide her consternation, she got out her checkbook and fumbled through her purse for a pen. Without looking at Letitia, she wrote out the check.

"Thank you," Letitia said, taking the check. She sounded suddenly stiff. Perhaps she'd read Tess's mind.

"You're welcome," Tess said, grabbing her purchase and departing in haste.

Letitia, Marlene, Rex. During the course of her excursion through the exhibition hall, the three people she'd talked to had risen to the top of her list as suspects in Cassie's murder. Tess was beginning to think that she'd lost all objectivity. She needed an outside opinion. Luke wasn't a good choice because he knew even less about these people than she did, and besides, he'd already accused her of spending too much time thinking about the murder. And Chief Butts would tell her to mind her own business.

There *was* one person who might be a help. Should she talk to Mary about her suspicions? After all, Mary knew Marlene, Letitia, and Rex much better than Tess did.

But she mustn't, as Luke said, go off half-cocked.

She decided to go home and think about it some more.

Chapter 17

On Sunday, it rained in torrents until mid-afternoon. Consequently, attendance at the final day of the quilt show was less than anticipated. The winner of the quilt guild's raffle wasn't even there when her ticket was drawn from the box. The prize quilt would be mailed to her.

By three o'clock, the hall was deserted except for the participants, who began packing up immediately. By five o'clock, everybody was gone except for Mary and Tess, who'd postponed dismantling the Drunkard's Path booth to help the other participants carry their unsold merchandise to their cars. For once, Tess wasn't hosting the traditional Sunday afternoon tea for her guests in the library in the tower of Iris House. She'd known she would be at the exhibition hall too late.

Looking around the deserted hall, Tess said wearily, "Where did the other guild members disappear to?"

"They were needed at home, couldn't miss evening church service, had to make dinner," Mary said. "One and all, they have good excuses."

"Of course they do," Tess said dryly. "Besides, you and I have nothing better to do."

Mary smiled. "The two of us got the booth ready for the show. I guess we can dismantle it." She began gathering up the few unsold pieces that remained and stuffing them into an open cardboard carton.

Tess tossed in the teddy bear and a couple of other props. "Be thankful for small favors," she said.

Mary straightened, planted an arm on her hip. "At the moment I can't think of one."

"We don't have to sweep the hall. Snodgrass can do it tomorrow—before he adds that guard rail to the loft."

Mary looked at the partitions that formed the back and two sides of the booth. "I suppose we should put these partitions back upstairs where we found them."

"Might as well," Tess agreed. "As a favor to Snodgrass. We can remind him of it next year when we need his help getting ready for the quilt show again."

Simultaneously they looked up at the high ceiling as the rain started again, sounding like the frenzied beating of a hundred jungle drums in the empty hall.

"We don't want to go out in that, anyway," Mary observed.

"See? Small favors," Tess observed.

They each grabbed one end of a partition and carried it toward the stairs. Mary went first, lifting the awkward partition from one step to the next, with Tess steadying it below.

Chief Butts had not put in another appearance at the show, and Tess had concluded that the investigation was stymied and the murder could well remain unsolved. It made her angry, knowing that somebody might get away with murder.

She pushed that thought aside for another. "Did you get a chance to talk to Marlene before she left?" she asked Mary as they set the partition on one side of the loft.

"Briefly."

Tess turned on the loft light and saw the tightness that had settled around Mary's mouth.

"She told me about—something she did a long time ago. I'm afraid we didn't part on very good terms."

Evidently Marlene had waited until the last minute to tell Mary how her name had gotten on Shannon Diamond's birth certificate. Tess felt sad for the two old friends. "Because of the birth certificate?" she asked.

Mary was heading for the stairs, but at Tess's question she turned back abruptly. "She told *you* before she told me?"

Tess shook her head. "She didn't tell me. I guessed."

"How did you do that?"

"The picture you have in your den—"

Mary looked blank.

"The one with the broken glass." Too late, Tess remembered that the picture had been in a drawer. She would never have seen it if she hadn't snooped. But she couldn't get around it now. "The drawer was partly open," she explained, "and the light reflected off the glass." Might as well make a clean breast of it. "I was curious, so I took it out."

Mary's hand closed on the iron-pipe banister. She said nothing.

Which embarrassed Tess and made her babble. "You know the one I mean, don't you? The picture taken of you and your husband and the Terhunes and Oxleys. Marlene said it was taken on a cruise to celebrate Cassie's promotion at the Hexler Corporation. Marlene's expression in the picture reminded me of someone else, but I didn't realize it was Shannon until later."

Mary was studying her in an odd way. Good grief, she'd merely looked in a drawer. It wasn't the crime of the century. But from Mary's demeanor, Mary thought otherwise. Tess decided the wisest thing to do was change the subject.

She walked toward the stairs. Mary started down and Tess followed. "I've been thinking," Tess said, "about the murder."

Mary didn't look around. "Oh?"

"I'm beginning to think Cassie was the intended victim, all along."

"Really?"

They had reached the bottom of the stairs. Tess walked briskly to the booth and grabbed hold of another partition. Mary followed more slowly, took her position on the other side. They carried it to the stairs and worked their way toward the loft slowly, as before.

Mary remained uncharacteristically silent. "Hey," Tess said, "you OK up there?"

Mary rested her end of the partition on a step for a moment. She closed her eyes briefly. "What makes you think Cassie was the intended victim?"

This particular conversational subject wasn't going any more smoothly than the previous one. Why had Mary turned so prickly all of a sudden? "Because she had enemies."

"And what about the fact that I was nearly killed by those boards falling off the loft?"

Tess shrugged. She hadn't really thought it all through. That's why she'd wanted to talk to Mary, to get her input. It had seemed like a good idea earlier. Now she wasn't so sure. "I suppose the boards could have been an accident."

They continued up another few steps with the partition. "A few days ago," Mary said finally, "you tried to convince me it *wasn't* an accident."

"Well . . . if it wasn't, then it was a diversionary tactic." They paused at the top of the stairs to catch their breath. After a moment, they set the partition out of the way.

"What does that mean?"

Tess looked at Mary. Something about the way she

stood, between Tess and the stairs, seemed alert, poised. Tess spoke before she realized the import of what she was saying. "The killer wanted it to look like you were the target. Then when he killed Cassie, people would think he'd killed the wrong person. And the investigation would go nowhere." Suddenly it struck her how like some of those mystery novels Nedra read it all sounded. In other circumstances, it might have been laughable. Except that some cases of reality could be as convoluted as fiction, and in that moment Tess sensed that this was one of those cases.

It was all so confusing. But she felt she was right, the killer had made it look as though he was after Mary Franks, when he'd really been after Cassie. So where did that lead? What did it tell her about the killer's identity?

Mary had seen no one in the loft or on the stairs when the boards fell.

Because the killer had run down the outside staircase?

Or because no one was there?

No one but Mary.

Tess's mind hovered on the brink of an impossible thought. Mary had been truly unnerved by the murder. Was that possible, if she herself had killed Cassie? Tess tried to think. It was difficult with Mary watching her. It had been dark when Cassie was killed. Perhaps the killer hadn't known how deeply affecting the sight of Cassie's bloody body would be until the lights came on and it was too late to do anything about it.

Oh, no, not Mary. Not sad, helpless Mary.

Mary hadn't moved, had scarcely breathed. Her eyes were narrowed on Tess. The silence was oppressive.

It dawned on Tess that she'd let her mouth run ahead of her brain. She pressed her fingers against her temples. She was so tired, but she knew she was close to understanding everything.

Mary watched her.

Not Mary, for God's sake. She had no motive.

Mary was in the rest room when the lights went out. Cassie had insisted that she go and lie down and had offered to take over the booth for a while. Marlene and Letitia had remarked that such solicitousness was unlike Cassie. So perhaps it hadn't happened that way at all. Perhaps Mary had pleaded illness and Cassie had had little choice but to take over the booth temporarily.

Still, Mary had been in the rest room when the lights went out.

But Shannon claimed that *she* was in the rest room and she hadn't seen Mary. Tess had assumed it was Shannon who was lying, but if Shannon wasn't the murderer, she'd have no reason to lie. Was it Mary who had lied?

And what about those boards? Could Mary have pushed them off, then run down the stairs and faked a fall before anybody could get within sight of her? Ordinarily, no. But Snodgrass had made a passageway of those tall partitions between the stairs and the quilt show booths. Tess had been the first to reach Mary, and it had taken her thirty seconds, perhaps a full minute, to get around the partitions to where she could see Mary.

And who had more opportunity than Mary to position that claw hammer on top of the booth partition so that it would appear to have been placed there to fall on Mary herself?

It was beginning to make a horrible kind of sense to Tess. Except for the why of it. Cassie was an old friend of Mary's and of Mary's late husband. When Cassie got that promotion in the Hexler Corporation, who did she want to celebrate with but her oldest friends, the Oxleys and the Franks.

Wait a minute.

Hadn't Luke mentioned the Hexler Corporation?

Think, Tess ordered herself. Cassie had worked as a corporate attorney for the Hexler Corporation. And Luke had said that Gerald Franks had killed himself because he was about to be indicted for insider trading in shares of—oh, dear God! The Hexler Corporation. Franks had acted on inside information given to him by a company source.

It all fell into place for Tess.

"Cassie," she breathed. "She was your husband's inside source in that stock scandal." She took a step toward the stairs.

Mary blocked her way. "I knew you couldn't resist snooping, that you'd think the killer was after me and tell the police. Everything worked out exactly as I'd planned. But you wouldn't stop. You just couldn't let it alone, could you, Tess? You had to keep snooping until you finally figured it out."

Tess could think of nothing to say. Mere words would not alter her situation now.

"It was *her* idea!" Mary said. "*She* came to Gerald, said they'd split whatever profit he made. But when the federal investigaors got on to her, she made a deal to testify."

When things turned out badly, she did whatever she had to do to keep herself out of trouble.

"Against Gerald? But he was her friend."

A nerve beside Mary's eye was twitching. "Cassie had to save her own skin. She couldn't be concerned with friends. So Gerald became her patsy. In exchange for her agreement to give up the practice of law and her promise to testify in court against Gerald, she wasn't prosecuted. I don't know why it took me nearly two years to figure out what really happened. With Cassie, it was always Cassie first and let the rest of the world be damned."

"Oh, Mary . . . I'm so sorry." Tess's mind was racing, seeking a way out. "I'll tell you what. We'll go to the police together. We'll explain the extenuating circumstances . . ."

"And they'll let me go?" Mary said disdainfully. "Sure they will. How dumb do you think I am, Tess?"

"They won't let you go, of course, but—" As she spoke, Tess had edged toward the door that led to the outside staircase. Now she grabbed the knob and turned. Nothing happened. It was locked.

"There's no other way out," Mary said triumphantly. Her eyes looked different. They glittered with cold, hard decision. This was a Mary Tess didn't know.

She froze for just an instant, then she forced herself to look at the woman she had thought was her friend, to speak calmly. "Don't make it worse than it already is, Mary." As suddenly as it had started, the rain stopped, leaving a menacing silence in its place.

Tess edged slowly toward the stairs—and Mary.

At that moment, Marlene Oxley stepped quietly into the hall and hesitated, looking around. Oh, thank heaven. "Marlene's here," Tess said loudly.

Marlene looked up at the sound of Tess's voice, but remained silent.

"Give it up, Tess. You can't trick me into looking away," Mary said in a deadly calm voice. "I can't let you go." She might have been commenting on a quilt pattern. "Because if you tell what you know, my daughter's life will be destroyed."

"You should have thought of that before you committed murder."

"Cassie had to pay for what she did to me!"

"And now, because of what you've done, Miranda will pay with years of heartbreak."

Mary's face twisted with fury. Tess bolted for the stairs.

Mary grabbed her arm. Tess struggled, but with a strength born of rage and desperation, Mary pulled her toward the edge of the loft. The sound of their heavy breathing filled the silence. They stared at each other.

Tess became aware that she stood only a few feet from the edge, her back to it.

Mary's intention was in her hard eyes and the grim set of her mouth. Oh, please, no . . .

As Mary braced herself, preparing to leap, Tess caught the faint change in her stance.

In the instant Tess's mind was telling her body to drop and roll to one side, Marlene spoke in a shocked voice. "Mary, what are you doing?"

Then everything seemed to happen at once.

As Tess rolled to one side, yelling, "Help, Marlene!" Mary lunged forward.

Mary's shocked cry mingled with Tess's anguished moan. Her hands grabbing the empty air frantically, Mary fell to the floor below. Tess heard Marlene's horrified wail. "Mary! Oh, my God, Mary!"

Tess crawled to the edge of the loft and looked down. Mary's body lay crumpled on the concrete. Marlene ran forward and knelt over her friend. "Mary, I had to come back. I have to make you understand why I did what I did. Please forgive me."

Finally, Marlene fell silent. Moments passed as Tess watched, paralyzed.

Marlene looked up, her face distorted by grief. "She's dead. I don't understand. She was trying to kill you."

A door banged open and Desmond Butts clumped into the exhibition hall on his crutches. "I'm here to arrest Mary Franks," he announced. Then he saw Mary's crumpled body. "What in God's name happened here?"

Chapter 18

Later, at the police station, Tess explained to Chief Butts in detail what had happened, with Marlene backing her up. Luke was there, too. Tess had called him before leaving the exhibition hall.

"How in tarnation did you figure out that Mary Franks was the killer?" Butts asked Tess.

"I almost didn't." Tess gave Butts an apologetic little shrug. "I'd stayed to help Mary dismantle the quilt guild's booth. I mentioned to Mary that I was beginning to think Cassie was the murderer's intended victim all along. I hoped that Mary could tell me who might have wanted to kill Cassie."

"She sure did that!" Butts sputtered.

"Not at first, but her reaction was so bizarre, it made me question all my conclusions."

"Kind of late," Butts put in.

Tess let that pass. "It occurred to me that Mary could have done it all. She could have pushed those boards off the loft and run downstairs before anyone saw her. There was just enough time. Both Shannon Diamond and Mary claimed they were in the ladies' rest room when the lights went out in the exhibition hall. I had been assuming that Shannon was lying. This afternoon, when I thought about it, I realized that the liar could as easily be Mary. Shannon didn't know Cassie. Mary did, which made it far more likely that she'd have a motive for murder. My mistake was speaking to Mary before I'd thought it through.''

"It almost got you killed," Luke reminded her. As if she could forget!

"If you'd waited, none of it would have happened," Butts said. "I'd have had her in jail.''

"What put you on to her, Chief?" Tess asked, wanting to divert his attention from her own actions.

"Her husband told me some things that gave me new leads to follow. Seems Cassie and Mary Franks's husband were in some kind of illegal stock deal together, and when they got caught, Cassie turned state's evidence to keep from being prosecuted herself.''

"I know," Tess said.

"You should have told me what you suspected and let me handle it," Butts muttered.

Tess shrugged. "By the time I'd worked it out, I'd already said too much to Mary. And I had no way of knowing that you'd already reached the same conclusion.''

Butts grumbled something incoherent.

Tess sighed. "I know what I should have done, Chief. If I'd waited, talked to you about it first, Mary wouldn't be dead now.'' Tess shivered.

Luke put his arm around her shoulders protectively.

Marlene, who had been listening silently, spoke up. "I'm not so sure. This morning when I talked to Mary, she seemed so weary. She said she couldn't get the sight of Cassie dead out of her mind. I think she was just beginning to comprehend that she would have to live the rest of her life with the knowledge of what she'd done. I'm not sure she could have managed it.''

"You may be right, Marlene," Tess said. "Mary hadn't managed very well so far. She stayed at home all day

Thursday. That was so out of character for her. I should have suspected something then.''

''But didn't she realize what it would do to Miranda if she found out what her mother had done?'' Luke asked.

Marleen shook her head. ''She probably convinced herself she was doing it for Miranda. Mary's daughter was the only thing she had to live for. I'm just saying, once she'd actually committed murder, I'm not sure even Miranda would have been enough.''

''I'd forgotten about Miranda,'' Tess said. ''That child has had to bear too much for her years. Does she know about her mother?''

''I called and told her there had been an accident, before I came to the station,'' Marlene said. ''She's with Kendra's family at their house now. I spoke to Kendra's mother, asked her to tell Miranda that Mary was dead. I just couldn't do it on the phone.''

Luke shook his head sadly. ''What will become of her?''

''I've been thinking about that,'' Marlene went on. ''I intend to ask her to come and live with Mike and me in Kansas City. She's known us all her life. I think she'd feel more at home with us than with anyone else.''

''That's very kind of you, Marlene,'' Tess said. Marlene caught Tess's gaze. In her eyes was the knowledge that she had a daughter of her own that she wanted to be a part of her future. Tess hoped Mike Oxley would support his wife in what she had to do.

Tess glanced at Chief Butts. ''Miranda is going to have a tough time of it, Chief. You could make it a little easier for her.''

''Me?'' Butts looked at her with a shocked expression. ''Kinda late to be asking for my help, isn't it?'' he asked sourly.

''Please, Chief,'' Tess pleaded. ''You must help that girl.''

"What can *I* do?"

"Miranda doesn't have to know that her mother was a murderer, does she?" Tess asked. "Mary's dead. What good will it do to broadcast it now?"

"Are you suggesting that I let Cassie Terhune's murder go down as unsolved?" he sputtered. "Withhold information? That's an actionable offense. You may be able to skirt the law while you play amateur sleuth, Tess Darcy. I don't have that luxury."

"All I'm suggesting is that you write your report and close the case as quietly as possible. If Miranda is in Kansas City, she won't know—unless you intend to let the newspapers get hold of all the gory details."

"The disposition of criminal cases is public information," Butts said, scowling fiercely.

"But you can use your considerable influence, Chief," Luke said smoothly.

Butts looked at Luke for a moment, then squared his shoulders. "Well . . . I can talk to the editor of the local paper, explain the situation, ask him to write the story so the girl will be protected."

"Thank you, that's very kind of you," Tess said. "I'm sure the editor will listen to you, Chief."

Butts looked down his nose at her.

"Tess," Luke put in, "you said that Mary only recently learned that Cassie had betrayed Gerald Franks. Did she say how she found out?"

"No. And she didn't say she'd learned it. Her exact words were that she'd 'figured it out.' "

"But how did she do that, two years after Gerald's suicide?" Luke asked.

"I think I know," Marlene said. "The other day, when I talked to Cassie's ex-husband, he mentioned that he'd phoned Mary a few weeks ago to see how she was getting along. I wasn't paying close attention at the time, but from something Ralph said, I realized later that he divorced Cassie because of something she'd done to Gerald Franks. Once I knew that, I understood what he meant. I think he must have said something similar to Mary. He probably assumed that Mary knew Cassie was Gerald's source in that stock scheme and that Cassie had made a deal with the federal investigators. Ralph wouldn't have stated it so baldly to Mary, but he probably alluded to it as he did when he talked to me. As I said, it wasn't until later that I understood what he meant. My guess is that whatever he said to Mary in that phone conversation, it set her thinking. And she worked it out, just as I did.''

Butts scanned their faces and grumbled, ''I'll get the stenographer in here to take your statements. Then''—he looked straight at Tess—''you can all go home and tend to your own business for a change.''

As Tess and Luke got into Luke's Jag, after leaving the station, Tess muttered, ''Would a simple 'are you all right' kill him?''

''Butts?''

''Of course Butts! I almost got myself killed getting Mary to confess!''

''If I were you, I wouldn't remind him. Right now, he's about as mad at you as he can be.''

Before Tess could respond, Luke closed her door and went around to the driver's side. After getting in, he reached out and took her hand and drew her near. ''I just want to look at you. You were almost killed today. If anything happened to you, Tess—''

''Nothing happened to me,'' she protested, her voice muffled against his shoulder.

''You thought it was going to, though, didn't you?''

Tess nodded, her forehead moving against the smooth cotton of his shirt. ''For a few minutes.''

"What am I going to do with you, my love?"

She lifted her head. "What are *you* going to do?" she demanded indignantly. "You do not make my decisions, Luke. I do! I am perfectly capable—"

He stopped her protest by kissing her. As his arms tightened around her. Tess had to admit that, for those few moments, it was nice to feel sheltered and protected in his arms.

Not that she had any intention of making it a way of life.

CHERRY-CREAM CREPES

Crepes: ¾ cup milk
½ cup all-purpose flour
1 egg
½ tablespoon cooking oil
⅛ teaspoon salt

In a bowl, combine milk, flour, eggs, oil, and salt. Beat with a rotary beater till well mixed. Heat a lightly greased 6-inch skillet. Remove from heat. Spoon in 2 tablespoons batter; spread batter evenly by tilting skillet. Return to heat; brown on one side only. Invert pan over paper towels; remove crepe. Repeat with remaining batter to make 8 or 9 crepes, greasing skillet occasionally.

Filling: 1 beaten egg
1 8-ounce package cream cheese, softened
2 tablespoons sugar
1 teaspoon vanilla

Beat together egg, cheese, sugar, and vanilla. Spoon 1 rounded tablespoon in center of unbrowned side of each crepe. Fold two opposite sides of crepe to center, then fold remaining two sides, overlapping edges. Place crepes in a 12x8-inch baking dish. Cover; heat in a 350-degree oven for 20 minutes or till hot.

Sauce: 1 can cherry pie filling

Heat pie filling in saucepan. Pour sauce over hot crepes and serve.

BROWNIE MUFFINS

¾ cup cocoa
1¼ cup butter or margarine
½ teaspoon butter extract
1½ cups chopped pecans or walnuts (optional)
1 cup flour
1¾ cups sugar
4 eggs, beaten
1 teaspoon vanilla extract
Powdered sugar (optional)

Preheat oven to 325 degrees. Melt butter over low heat in a saucepan. Add cocoa, butter extract, and chopped nuts (if you use them). Stir well. Remove from heat and set aside. Combine flour, sugar, eggs, and vanilla in a large mixing bowl; add cocoa mixture, stir until moistened. The batter will be very thin, like syrup. Spoon about 3 tablespoons (or use a ¼ cup measuring cup) of batter into paper-lined muffin pans. Bake at 325 degrees for 30 to 35 minutes or until muffins test done. Cool in pan for 10 minutes. Remove and sprinkle with powdered sugar, if desired. Makes about 18 muffins.

SCRUMPTIOUS CHOCOLATE CHIP COOKIES

½ cup granulated sugar
½ cup packed brown sugar
½ cup (1 stick) butter or margarine, softened
½ cup creamy peanut butter
1 teaspoon vanilla
1 egg
1 cup flour
½ cup quick-cooking or regular oats
1 teaspoon baking soda
⅓ teaspoon salt
1 cup semisweet chocolate chips

Preheat oven to 350 degrees. Beat together sugars, butter, peanut butter, vanilla, and egg until creamy. In a separate bowl, mix flour, oats, baking soda, and salt. Work flour mixture into sugar and butter mixture, then add chocolate chips.

Drop by heaping tablespoon about 2 inches apart on ungreased cookie sheet. Bake at 350 degrees about 10–12 minutes, until golden brown. Cool 4–5 minutes before removing from cookie sheet.

TESS'S CHICKEN-NOODLE CASSEROLE

1 can cream of chicken soup
1/2 cup milk
5 ounce can boned chicken
5 ounce package noodles (about 2 1/2 cups cooked)
1/4 cup buttered whole wheat bread crumbs
1/2 small (8-ounce) can English peas (optional)

Preheat oven to 375 degrees. Cook noodles according to package directions; drain. Blend soup and milk. Add chicken and noodles. Add peas (if desired). Spoon into casserole dish and sprinkle with crumbs. Bake at 375 degrees for 25 minutes.

JILL CHURCHILL

> "Agatha Christie is alive and well and writing mysteries under the name Jill Churchill."
> *Nancy Pickard*

Delightful Mysteries Featuring Suburban Mom Jane Jeffry

GRIME AND PUNISHMENT
76400-8/$4.99 US/$6.99 CAN

A FAREWELL TO YARNS
76399-0/$5.50 US/$7.50 CAN

A QUICHE BEFORE DYING
76932-8/$4.99 US/$6.99 CAN

THE CLASS MENAGERIE
77380-5/$4.99 US/$5.99 CAN

A KNIFE TO REMEMBER
77381-3/$4.99 US/$5.99 CAN

FROM HERE TO PATERNITY
77715-0/$4.99 US/$6.99 CAN